D1525895

AEP Urban Fiction
and
Hood Salidafied Publications
Presents

Brooklyn Sexy

Part 1

Myles Ramzee and Niko

Brooklyn Sexy Part 1
All Right Reserved.
Copyright © 2015 Myles Ramzee and Niko
Cover Design by Angela Stevenson-Ringo

Angel Eyes Publications
P.O. Box 22031 Beachwood, Ohio
angeleyespublications@yahoo.com

ISBN-13: 978-0692285978
ISBN-10: 0692285970
LCCN: 2014919892

AEP Urban Fiction is a Division of Angel Eyes Publications

Chapter 1

Diondre

"The categories are Candles, Sandals and Scandals." Diondre and Cornbread looked at each other confused.

"What?" Diondre, the dark chocolate skinned of the three asked. Diondre was raised in a house full of women; three sisters with him being the only boy. Diondre did not like his sisters being the prey of men like Shamar and vowed to never be like Shamar when it came to relationships, so he was a one woman man. Diondre was also the bookworm out of the trio. He was extremely smart, a straight A student from elementary all the way to high school. He loved to read. His favorite topic was Black history; something they didn't teach in Thomas Jefferson High. Though Diondre didn't like Shamar's way with women, he still considered Shamar his best friend. Shamar always had Diondre's back with anything. When people would try to pick a fight with Diondre by calling him a "nerd" or a "lame" Shamar would step up and fight anybody who insulted Diondre. Plus they say opposites attract.

"It's like this. A candle is the chick you can have a romantic candle light dinner with and bring home to meet yo peoples. You know, the type you wife. Sandals are shoes you can slip in and out of with ease, the girls who just wants to fuck. She's in and out of different beds with different dudes. Now the Scandals are the typical Brooklyn chick. She's a boosting, credit card scamming, weed smoking, materialistic, spend her welfare check on getting her hair and nails done chick that will set you up to get robbed by some grimy ass Brooklyn nigga." Shamar's breakdown had Cornbread nodding his head in agreement while Diondre stood there shaking his head in disbelief.

"Yo, you crazy man I swear." Diondre muttered.

"It's true yo!" Shamar blurted.

"Nah man your typical Brooklyn chick isn't in your scandals category son. I got three sisters all older than me one in college, one is a law student, my sister Shante is a housewife to the man who took her virginity and Nicky works for Corrections, never been on welfare, boosted, smoke weed or set anybody up. My mother was born and raised in Bed Stuy and she was nothing like you say a typical Brooklyn chick is." Diondre said matter of factly.

"Hey Dre our families don't count." Shamar said.

Again, Diondre shook his head. "Son you crazy for real, stop smoking that weed."

That night when Diondre laid in his bed after reading *"Sex and Race"* by J. A. Rogers he thought about which of Shamar's three categories his girlfriend of two months Deidre fit in. She lived in the projects but she wasn't a weed smoking, boosting and all that crazy stuff type of woman that

Shamar put in his scandals category. They hadn't had sex yet so she wasn't the sandal type, but was she the candle type Diondre asked himself. Then he began to giggle at the thought of it.

"Yo Shamar done bumped his head." Diondre pulled his quilt over his head and went to sleep.

Chapter 2

Deidre

"OOOH girl I'm hating, ya'll got flat screens, DVD players, video games and all that up in this joint."

"Bitch please you know damn well you're gonna be all up in here tryna sell us stuff you done boosted or got on somebody credit." Deidre joked to her Puerto Rican friend who favored the sexy Rocsi from B.E.T's 106 and Park. Her name is Elizabeth but everyone called her Liz. Though Deidre said it jokingly, there was no doubt in her mind that Liz would do exactly what she joked about. Sell boosted clothes to the customers.

"Anyway...." Liz said with attitude in her unmistakable Brooklyn accent. Liz's accent made her sound like Rosie Perez.

"Ya'll doing it big Dee. I'm happy for you. You always were the lucky one to find a good man. You know how hard it is to find a good man especially round here," Liz said seriously while admiring the salon.

Deidre hated to admit it but Liz was right. She was lucky.

These days men like Diondre were scarce and most of the times the good ones out there were taken. A lot of good black men are developing into these "trophies" while sitting behind bars wasting away leaving out in the free world a bunch of lonely, horny, some even desperate women who needed a good intelligent strong black man in their lives.

Deidre smiled when she thought of Diondre, her knight in shining armor, the man who swept her off her feet in high school and made her somewhat rough life easier. A man who looked deep within her instead of just focusing on her five-five, cute in the face, slim in the waist, thick in the right place frame. Diondre was the man who took her out of the projects and into a refurbished colonial style brownstone in the Fort-Greene section of Brooklyn.

"Liz you can do it big too. All you gotta do is save some money and stay out of jail."

Deidre said holding Liz's shoulders so she could face her.

"Dee please don't get all Malcolm X on me now. I make do with my babysitting gig and doing hair on the side. It ain't all about stealing and shit." Liz shot back.

"What if I told you me and Diondre want you to work here," Deidre said with a big smile. Liz put her hands over her mouth in shock.

"Don't play Dee, you fa real?"

"Serious as cancer," Deidre replied with one hand on her chest and one raised as if she were giving a scouts oath.

"But I thought Diondre wasn't so fond of me."

"What gave you that idea?" Deidre asked as if she were clueless, when in reality at one point Diondre didn't like Liz. He thought she was what his friend Shamar described as, "a typical Brooklyn girl" in one of his crazy categories but as Diondre got to know Liz he begin to understand why she was the way she was.

Elizabeth "Liz" Calderon was born out of wedlock to a mother who constantly was high off heroine and a drunken father who wound up in a crazy home after mysteriously losing his mind.

Liz raised herself by fixing her own breakfast and dinner, which she had to steal from the local C-Town, and she clothed herself by becoming one of Bruekelen project's best thieves. Her mother spent all of her money getting high, to keep her off the streets and winding up dead in a filthy shooting gallery, Liz purchased her mother's fixes for her every morning and night. When Liz turned eighteen, she came home one day from boosting and found her mother naked and dead from an overdose. At the time; Liz was receiving social security checks from the government due to her father's illness and was on the lease of the project apartment. Social Security paid the rent. Being a thief was all she knew.

The one thing that made Diondre nervous about Deidre's friendship with Liz was the company Liz kept. All of Liz friends except Deidre were boosters and scammers. Something Diondre constantly reminded Deidre of.

"You're the only one of her friends that's not scandalous and the guys she has around are some shady dudes. Stay away from them."

"Will you let it go Dre I swear sometimes I believe Shamar's spirit has invaded your body."

Deidre didn't believe Diondre was possessed by Shamar's spirit but she knew his tragic death was something Diondre had a hard time getting over and Deidre was there to help Diondre get through it just like he was there for her when her father died suddenly from walking pneumonia.

***

1990

"I can't wait to graduate. That is all my grandmom said I gotta do and I can move back uptown with her. I can't take this Brooklyn shit."

"Sha, why do you hate Brooklyn so much?" Diondre asked Shamar as they walked out of the Time Square Store (T.S.S) towards their East New York neighborhood.

"It's not that I hate it. It's just boring yo. You can't find a decent chick you can trust. You can't get any real money, and these niggas out here are on some bullshit. You wanna know what's the worst part though? You can't find no real good weed."

Diondre couldn't identify with Shamar's feelings towards his beloved birthplace. Diondre found a decent chick, he didn't smoke weed and he didn't hustle but to Diondre there was no place like Brooklyn. He didn't have to leave Brooklyn for anything. There were plenty of places to go shopping for clothes that were in style. You could go downtown to Fulton Street mall or Albee Square mall. Shop, eat and catch a movie at the Metro. You could go to Junior's for its famous cheesecake.

As a kid, Diondre remembered his parents bringing him and his sisters to Coney Island's Astroland Park and there was nothing like a Nathan's frank with the hot French fries with melted cheese on them.

Then during the summer, you could go to the boys and girls high school for the Annual African Street festival and enjoy a whole day of African American, Caribbean and African culture. There were hundreds of vendors selling everything from African clothing and jewelry to different varieties of cultural food. That was Diondre's favorite place to go. It was a day that made him proud to be a black man from Brooklyn.

During Labor Day, you could head to Eastern Parkway and enjoy the West Indian Day parade. It was Brooklyn's version of Carnival. Boy that's a thing to see!

Diondre remembered the days his father would take him and his sisters on bike rides through Prospect Park, stop at the Zoo then head across the street to the Botanical Gardens. Diondre cherished those days. Brooklyn is the birthplace of some famous and infamous people.

It is the birthplace of Michael Jordan, Mike Tyson, Nia Long and Chris Rock. The Major league baseball's color barrier was broke here with Jackie Robinson playing for the Brooklyn Dodgers. The rappers Notorious B.I.G, Jay-Z and Lil Kim are Brooklynites. The infamous gangsta Alphonse Capone fled Brooklyn on the run from the law. He was born and raised on these streets and ran with a gang known as the Fulton Rockaway boys. The mafia's most vicious gang of killers was spawned in most populated borough of New York City, murder incorporated. The man responsible for practically dismantling New York five mafia families Rudolph Giuliani was born in this borough.

What else could be said? Brooklyn, a name derived from the Canarsie Indians meaning, "Broken Land" is a place with 2.5 million stories to tell. You gotta love it!

It's too bad Shamar didn't get a chance to experience all he could of Brooklyn. A week before graduation, Shamar was riding the A train on his way back to Brooklyn after visiting his grandmother in Harlem. He had just returned from a shopping spree on Broadway and 96th street. He wore a Gucci link necklace, a Gucci link bracelet and a brand new leather jacket over a black college hooded sweater. When the train stopped at Rockaway Avenue Shamar noticed two sneaky looking dudes get on the train. They immediately stared at Shamar and Shamar, trying to look intimidating, stared back menacingly. The two guys grinned at Shamar who didn't return the grin. When the train stopped at Pitkin Avenue Shamar got off and so did the two guys both wearing camouflaged army fatigues. Shamar walked as if he had no care in the world but he was nervous. He knew by the way they looked and where he was, that nine times out of ten these guys were looking for trouble.

Once outside the train station on Pitkin Avenue, Shamar realized he shouldn't have got off at the dark, desolate and dilapidated part of East New York. That's when he heard the all too familiar sound of a gun being cocked and a voice behind him saying.

"A yo money where you from?"

"Fuck," Shamar mumbled to himself as he turned to face his assailants, to his utter dismay, they both had guns. One had a large nickel-plated gun that reflected off the street light and the other was a black revolver looked like a 44 Bulldog.

"I'm from Harlem," Shamar heard himself say. He almost tried to catch his tongue but it just came out. Telling these Brooklyn guys he was from Harlem was equivalent of begging them to rob him.

"Run yo shit mister Harlem," one of the guys ordered making the other one chuckle.

"Yo son you hear this herb talking bout Harlem. He said that shit like it meant something." One of the robbers snorted.

Shamar removed his coat and handed it to one of the guys who had his gun pointed at Shamar's chest while the other pointed his towards Shamar's lower body looking around making sure no one could see the drama unfolding.

"Everything nigga," the guy with the gun pointing at Shamar's chest said sticking the gun into Shamar's chest. "The Jordan's too."

"C'mon black don't make me..." Shamar was cut off.

"Yo clap this nigga son!" Boc! Boc! Boc! The guy shot Shamar three times in his chest before

Shamar fell to the ground. Then shockingly the guy stood over Shamar and... Boc! Boc! Boc! Shot Shamar in his face. Both men removed Shamar's jewelry and money out of his pocket. Then before leaving, one of them removed Shamar's Air Jordan's. "Cmon Son!"

The guys fled into the night and were never apprehended. Shamar lay in an East New York gutter for hours until a cop walking the beat saw his bloody body laying there. He spoke into his walkie-talkie nonchalantly. "Oh seven five, this is two-seven-eight..."

"Come in two-seven-eight," the dispatched responded.

"I'm gonna need an ambulance and probably the morgue to come pick up a body. I'm on Pitkin and Barbey."

"10-4."

Chapter 3

Deidre

"Dre I was just telling Liz about me and you wanting her to work here."

"Dre thank you so much. I swear on my mother's grave you won't be disappointed. I'm going to have this place poppin' yo. Watch," Liz said excitedly. Dre hugged Liz and over her shoulder, he raised his eyebrows at Deidre.

"I know you will Liz, trust me I know."

"Oooh turn that Ne-yo joint up that's my joint!" Liz walked off singing.

***

Liz

A week after the shop open the place was up and running as if it's been open for years. All the women in the projects came to get their hair done and Deidre's friends from her days at Columbia University came in to get pampered. The shop offered facials of all sort. Diondre hired five barbers and Deidre hired four hair stylists including Liz. All of Liz customers she had before the shop now came there to get their hair done. Of course her boosting buddies stopped by to off the clothes they boosted. Liz showed love to her former crime partners and purchased clothes from them. Even Diondre couldn't resist some of the items they bought in for men. The Tru Religion was some of his favorites, along with some Antik denim. He even purchased some seven jeans for Deidre.

Deidre couldn't remember seeing Liz so happy. Liz's happiness made Deidre happy. Deidre knew Liz felt the same for her. Deidre always smiled at how happy Liz was for her when she and Diondre first hooked up.

***

Back in High School

The lunchroom in Thomas Jefferson was jam packed with students standing around in groups, some beating on tables while another sang a rap by Public Enemy or Rakim. Some students battled it out with their own raps. People flirted while some couples held hands planning to sneak in one of the bathrooms for some teen sex. Groups of thugs bopped around looking for trouble, intimidating the students who happened to be in school to actually learn.

"That guy from the private houses likes you Dee," Liz said as her and Deidre sat at a table listening to their walkmans.

"Who?" Deidre asked removing her headphones from her ears.

"Don't make it seem so obvious that we talkin' bout him, but he's at the table where those private house bitches be sitting at." Liz mumbled.

Deidre tried to play it off as cool as she could by turning her head acting as if she was just looking around. When she looked at the table where the guy sat, she caught him staring dead at her.

"You talkin' bout Dre? He's in my biology class. What makes you think he likes me?"

"This ain't the first time I saw him staring at you. Every time he sees you he starts staring like a groupie. Plus he the nigga from the private houses that is cool with people from the projects." Liz said.

"You make it seem like project people are like refugees or something," Deidre shot back. Liz sucked her teeth. "Anyway, he's cute, smart and he ain't nothing like these wannabe gangstas in this school."

"He aiight" Deidre said nonchalantly as if she didn't find him that attractive though she did.

"Shoo, if you don't want him I'll damn sure give him some," Liz snorted.

Deidre rolled her eyes at Liz. "Ho you'll give the principal some if he wanted."

Liz playfully hit Deidre on her shoulder. "Shut up bitch."

When classes resume the students poured out into the hallway, Diondre approached Deidre and Liz.

"Excuse me Deidre. Can I get a word in with you?" He asked in a soft polite tone.

"Get yours girl," Liz mumbled walking off.

Deidre couldn't front, Diondre had it going on with his dark smooth skin, high cheek bones made him look sort of exotic, his chinky eyes were sexy and his wavy hair was shaped up sharply. He stayed in something by Polo. Deidre thought he was one of those Lo-life guys; a gang of youth from different parts of Brooklyn who wore nothing but Polo clothing from head to toe they were infamous for boosting or the smash and grab. Diondre didn't run with those types. He only hung out with his two friends Shamar and his chubby stepbrother Cornbread. Still, Deidre didn't think he was her type.

"What words do you wanna get in with me?" Deidre said acting as if Diondre was interrupting some important place or thing she had to get to.

"I'll get right to the point." Diondre said.

"Please do, I have a class to get to," Deidre said with a cocky tone. Diondre had a feeling it was a front, a hard to get act. She didn't want to appear easy.

"I wanna take you to a movie some time, whenever you can go."

"Why you wanna take me to a movie? Why don't you go with one of those private house girls you live around?" Deidre said with attitude.

"Whoa! You got me mixed up with some other dude. I don't live around those girls. I live in Linden Plaza." Diondre said matter-of-factly.

"What's the difference? Linden plaza, the private houses it's all the same. I thought us project girls weren't good enough for ya'll." Deidre grunted.

"Where you live has no meaning to me.

What's important to me is who you are and that's who I wanna get to know. I don't wanna meet the building you live in."

Deidre was impressed. She never heard a guy say things like he said. Usually when a guy tried to talk to her and they would find out she was a project girl, their whole attitude would change. They would either think she was willing to go in the bathroom with them to have sex or they would cut the conversation short altogether. The stereotype of most project girls was that they were fast and quick to set a dude up to be robbed.

"If I don't have something to do this weekend maybe I'll go with you to the movies," Deidre said causing a big smile to appear to Diondre's face. She adored his smile.

"Can I call you then?" Diondre asked.

"Uh uh give me your number I'll call you." Deidre snapped.

Diondre quickly removed a small piece of paper with his number on it and handed it to Deidre.

"Damn you just knew I was gonna ask for your number or something?"

Diondre felt embarrassed.

"I'll wait for your call." Diondre said. Deidre nodded her head then went looking for Liz.

Deidre looked in Liz class and didn't see her there. "Where is this girl?" Deidre mumbled to herself. Deidre had to pee so she went to the bathroom that was located at the bottom floor of the school.

When she pushed the door open to one of the stalls her eyes widened at the scene unfolding in front of her. There in plain view was Liz with her jeans down to her right ankle sitting on one of the biggest dicks Deidre ever saw while the guy sat on the toilet.

"Dee closed the door!" Liz panted. Deidre let the door close hearing Liz moan. "Ooh Shamar fuck me poppy!"

That weekend Deidre called Diondre and she agreed to go to the movies with him. He picked her up in a cab and they went to Kings Plaza. During the movie Diondre paid attention to Deidre's facial features than he did the actual movie.

"Why are you staring at me?" Deidre whispered.

"I can't believe how pretty you are," Diondre whispered back. After thanking him, Deidre grabbed his chin and turned it towards the screen. "Watch the movie boy." Diondre laughed then he watched the movie. Afterwards Diondre wanted to take her to eat at IHOP but after Deidre got off the phone with her mother and father that plan was nixed.

"My mother and father said I got to go home," Deidre said sadly.

Disappointed Diondre replied. "It's cool... I'll see you at school Monday."

They rode in the cab in silence all the way to Deidre's building. When the car stopped Deidre reached over and gave Diondre a soft kiss on his cheek. "Call me." Deidre said before exiting the vehicle.

The next day early in the morning Deidre went to Liz's apartment to tell her about her date. First Deidre had to address the bathroom episode.

She hasn't seen Liz since that day because Liz was spending a few days at her grandmother's house in Bushwick. Really, house sitting while her grandmother flew to Puerto Rico for a few days. It was a cool arrangement for Liz because she was free to do what she wanted for almost week. If you give Liz, free reign to your house for more than a day, there's no telling what she would do.

Liz answered the door half sleep. She opened the door and just turned around walking towards her bedroom. She had a long t-shirt on with nothing on under it and a red scarf on her head.

"Wassup girl. Guess who I went to the movies with?" Deidre said excited. Liz gave an inaudible mumble then fell flat on the bed.

"Get up Liz you act like you hung over or something. Is you?"

"No I'm tired leave me alone," Liz said in a groggy voice.

"I went out with that boy Diondre. He ain't from the private houses either he from Linden Plaza." Deidre said not getting a response from Liz.

"Did you hear me Liz I went out with Dre?"

"Can he fuck good?" Liz managed to mumble.

"Oh no you didn't. I didn't fuck him, I just met him unlike yo nasty ass. What was up with you and that boy Shamar in the bathroom? If a nigga will fuck you in that nasty bathroom he don't care anything about you." Deidre scolded.

Liz turned her head on the bed to face Deidre. "Fuck you Dee. I ain't care about his ass either I just wanted to see if it's what them other bitches in school say it was and damn it was."

Deidre shook her head. "Girl you need help."

Liz got up and went into the bathroom. Deidre could hear her throw up, then wash up and brush her teeth. When Liz came out of the bathroom, she was not the groggy, hung over Liz. She was up with a new found energy.

"I just needed to throw up. That gin fucked me up girl. Dee I'm sorry I asked did you fuck him. I know you ain't like that girl. I'm glad you went out with him, he seems real nice."

"He is nice. He ain't even tried to kiss me." Deidre said.

Liz gave her a confused look. "He didn't try to kiss you, what type of gay shit is that?"

Deidre sucked her teeth. "It's not gay it's respectful."

"Fuck is you Mother Theresa? Ain't nothing wrong with a kiss. Shit I need to see if a nigga can kiss before we go any further. Cause if he can't kiss he probably doesn't eat pussy and a bitch needs this pussy licked like a stamp," Liz grumbled.

"You going to hell," Deidre said.

"Shit hopefully the spit on my pussy from a niggas tongue will put the fire out."

Still in all Liz was happy for Deidre especially when Deidre and Diondre became an item. Deidre even wrote it on the wall in the girl's bathroom at their school. She wanted all the girls in the school to know that Diondre Sebastian Taylor was her man and he was off limits.

"Hey Debby what's good with you girl?" Liz

said excitedly as one of her customers walked in the shop. Liz looked at the expression on Deidre's face change as she spotted Debby walk in. There was always tension between the two and Liz thought the reason these girls hated each other was petty.

"Liz what's poppin' ma. I'm good as usual doing my thang," Debby said cutting her eyes at Deidre. Deidre had asked Liz before not to do Debby's hair in the shop but Liz explained since she worked in the shop her schedule wouldn't allow her to do Debby's hair anywhere else. Reluctantly Deidre let it be but just the sight of Debby ruined her day.

Debra Clarkson lived on the far side of Bruekelen projects, blocks away from Deidre and Liz's building. They knew each other from elementary school, junior high and high school and as little kids, they played on the same playgrounds in the projects but like most projects in New York City; the people in the neighborhood grow apart and it becomes like two separate neighborhoods. One side of the projects not liking the people from the other side that was a reality Deidre was more than happy to move away from.

Deidre and Debby's situation was a little different. Their fallout came over a boy. When they were in junior high school a boy from the far side everyone knew as "Web" short for Webster, a name he hated, liked Deidre. Deidre liked him too and they would pass each other notes in class.

Web sent her a note asking if she would go out with him and to mark the boxes yes or no he put in the letter. Deidre marked yes and they were boyfriend and girlfriend. They never got as far as a kiss when Deidre walked in the girl's bathroom and saw Web and Debby kissing.

Deidre immediately rushed towards Debby swinging and clawing. Unfortunately, Deidre was no match for Debby. Debby, a little bigger than Deidre, tore into Deidre until Web broke it up. With a bloody nose and her hair looking like, she got an electrical shock Deidre told Web: "I hate you. I hate both of you!"

Deidre ran home to her mother known in the neighborhood as Miss Knotts and cried while telling her about her ordeal. Miss Knots who Deidre was a splitting image of, told her twelve year old daughter. "You have to experience a broken heart so you'll know when your heart isn't broken."

Mrs. Knots laid in bed that night with her husband a hulk of a man who resembled Jim Brown in complexion and size barked. "Who is this boy, I'll break his arms."

"Melvin please if some poor girl's father were to break something on you for the hearts you broke you would have one bone left in your body. Now go to sleep."

That was 18 years ago and Deidre still hated Debby. It wasn't just about the heartbreak; it was more of a bruised ego. Not only did Debby take her new boyfriend but she also whooped her ass doing it and then bragged to everyone that she did. That really damages a person's pride.

Every time she saw Debby, it reminded her of

that terrible chapter in her life. Deidre told herself she should be mature enough to let bygones be bygones. They were kids and now Deidre had a good man who loved her, a successful man, and with her success as a college graduate with a degree in cosmetology and literature. Web and Debby thing should have been blown over. But fuck that, that bitch really kicked my ass and bragged, Deidre told herself and she wouldn't let it go.

"I got some seven jeans at my crib, citizens of humanity and some rock and republic joints I know you would like. Come take a look when you got time." Debby said as she sat in the chair to get her hair shampooed.

"Oh you know I will." Liz uttered excitedly.

"What's up with them phones and iPod's you were telling me about?" Liz inquired.

"Oh yeah got those too. Come up real big with these cards. Shit girl you don't know what you missing." Debby snorted with her eyes closed as Liz rubbed the herbal essence shampoo in her hair.

"I'm cool Deb. I needed a break from that. I'm tired of calling for bail all the way in Vegas. Sitting up for months until somebody came to get me. That shit wearing a bitch down," Liz explained

"I feel you. I'm thinking bout chilling too. Especially now that Web is home." Debby said. Deidre tried to act as if she wasn't listening to their conversation but of course she was. Deidre didn't know why but hearing that Web was finally out of jail after serving almost 11 years for a murder made her heart skip a beat. The last time she saw Web was in 1996 when her and Liz went to the Source Awards. She saw Web but Web didn't see her and from the way Web was looking like he didn't appear to be at the awards to enjoy the show.

He looked like he was up to no good. He was dressed in black fatigues with a black ski hat on his head. He was staring at guys walking in the theater menacingly. It was no secret that Web was a stick up kid. In fact, his name rang bells throughout Brooklyn as a vicious stick up kid. He was rumored to have robbed over fifty drug dealers, not small time dealers either, big-time dealers throughout the city. His method was to kidnap torture and kill his victims after receiving the money and the drugs. He was at the Source Awards targeting the rappers with the most expensive jewelry and the other ballers who attended the event. Deidre didn't say a word she just went on about her business.

"Word? When he get out?" Liz asked.

"Last week. He staying in a shelter cause parole didn't want him back in the projects being that the project was the scene of the crime." Debby answered in a sad tone.

Most girls in the shop heard Debby. Most of them also knew that she really didn't care about Web. She didn't do the time with him while he was away and she went and had a baby by this drug dealer from Red Hook projects and was still seeing him whenever he felt like playing the daddy role and having sex with her big booty self.

One thing the girls in the shop had to admit was that Debby was a very pretty, voluptuous girl, flat tummy, slim waist with an ass to make Buffy the body say damn and to top it all, she was a good mother. Her son had all that a child could get. She put him in a private school, paid for him to take Karate classes and took him on lots of trips. The only thing missing in that child's life was a daddy that loved him unconditionally.

One thing was for sure; Deidre hoped Debby wouldn't bring Web with her next time she came into the shop. Deidre didn't think she could stand seeing both of them together in the same room. It would give her flashbacks to that ass whooping in the bathroom.

Chapter 4

Debra

Ding-Dong Ding Dong, Ding Dong, Ding Dong!

"Hold up shit. Who the fuck ringing my damn door like they crazy?" Debra said in a groggy voice while wrapping her silk kimono style robe around her naked body. The silk hugged her large round bottom that jiggled as she walked to the door. She had her freshly done micro braids wrapped in a colorful silk scarf.

"What time is it anyway?" she mumbled as she looked through her peephole. Her attitude immediately changed when she saw who was at the door.

"Hey Web. 1 forgot you were coming over this morning." She said in an inviting tone.

She reached out to hug him and he walked past her to get in the house. "Damn, I don't get a hug nigga?"

Web stared at her for a few seconds, his body language read, is she serious? But instead he gave her a hug. He felt her nakedness under the soft robe and immediately felt a tingle in his crotch. Since he had been home he had a few sexual encounters with girls he met at the shelter he was staying at on Linden Boulevard. He didn't touch Debra and after doing 11 years without her even as much as writing him, he wanted no parts of her. The only reason he was dealing with her at all was because he had a plan.

"I'm going take a shower, you want some breakfast? I'm making some French toast, home fries and turkey sausage." Debra said while walking towards her bedroom.

From the first time Debra saw Web upon his release from jail she wanted to feel him inside of her. She knew it had been a while since she saw or even heard from him but seeing him again bought back old feelings and what made it hard for her not to feel that way was he looked very good. His dark skin had a smooth shiny glow. His waves were spinning like crazy and his body. Damn!

The nigga had it going on. His muscular body from all that iron pressing in the prison yard was bulging against his tank top and white-tee. When Debra hugged him the hardness of his body had her pussy throb and wet. Remembering how well endowed he was... she couldn't wait to have his dick up in her.

"Yeah that's cool. I don't eat meat though just leave the sausage off my plate," Web said in his baritone voice.

When Debra came out of the shower ten minutes later she had a lavender towel wrapped around her body and Web couldn't help but stare at her ass bouncing under it, with her bowed legs and small pedicure feet. Web grabbed his crotch feeling a hard-on coming on. Then Debby reached in her living room closet and purposely let the towel drop from off her body.

"Oh shit damn," she said turning to face Web to see if he was looking he was. Her 32 D's bounced as she bent to pick her towel up. Her stomach was flat and toned despite her having a baby. Web couldn't resist.

"Debby come here girl," he said seductively. Debby walked over to him holding on to her towel. She stood in front of him as he sat on her leather couch. "Wassup Web Lemme hurry up and get dressed so I can..."

Debra stopped talking as Web pulled her down to him removing her towel. He kissed her on her mouth passionately pushing his tongue down her throat. Her tongue met his as he palmed her soft, round ass still wet from her shower. Debby threw one of her legs around Webs waist. He placed one of his fingers in her wet slit and rubbed on her swollen clit. Debby moaned while gyrating her hips. She reached down unbuckling Webs pants. She reached in his pants stroking his erection.

Kissing Debby passionately, Web removed his pants and boxers releasing his anaconda to the jungle between Debby's thighs.

"Oh my God Web, fuck this pussy," Debby grunted as Web's pole pushed deep within Debby's opening. The warmness and wetness of her middle caused Web to let out a soft moan.

When Debby made the muscle in her pussy grip Web's manhood he had to bite his lip to stop himself from letting out a moan loud enough for the neighbors to here.

Debby rode his eleven inches like a pro. His love muscle touched every part of her insides causing her to cum multiple times, sending her juices flowing down Webs shaft onto his balls. Debby turned her back towards him to ride him giving him a lovely view of her dark brown, large bottom go up and down on him. He squeezed her cheeks as she rode.

"Damn Deb. This shit is good ma." Web mumbled. Debby reached between her legs to massage Web's wet balls. Webs toes curled as she did that. He could feel himself about to erupt.

"Oh shit I'm bout to nut Deb!" When Web started stroking faster Debby knew he was about to cum she turned around and bent between his legs placing his large organ in her mouth and began stroking him.

"AAH. AAH Shiiit!" Web grunted as he exploded in Debby's mouth with her swallowing every bit of it.

Afterwards Debby got dressed and fixed them breakfast. Web sat at her kitchen table admiring the decor of Debby's apartment. She had state of the art stereo equipment, flat screen T.V hung up on her living room wall and wall-to-wall carpeting. The crib was decked out.

"You really laced this crib Deb. What happen to your apartment in the projects?" Web asked as Debby placed a steaming plate in front of him.

"When my mom moved down south my little sister and her baby father stayed there. "Deb answered taking a seat across from him.

"You still had to be close to the projects though huh. So you move over here in the private houses?" Web chuckled causing Deb to giggle also. Debby's apartment was a two-story home on 106st and Flatlands Avenue directly across the street from the projects. Debby had the 1st floor apartment while a Jamaican couple live in the second floor.

"You know I'm a Bruekelen girl to the heart. Plus, most of my customers and friends are there. Don't front nigga if parolc allowed you, you'd be right back on Williams Avenue with your grandmother."

"Where's your son?" Web asked changing the subject. Two years after Web went to jail Debby gave birth to a beautiful baby boy she named after her baby father. Little Ty-Ran was now ten years old. Web heard about it while he was in Green Haven Correctional facility from a young cat from the projects that was sent there. Though Web was hurt he didn't show it outwardly. He kept it to himself. Before he went to jail, he was in love with Debby and from the way it looked, she was in love with him too. She had got his name tattooed on her ankle. She kept his picture in her purse everywhere she went and all she talked about in school was Web this, Web that; until he got locked up. Once she heard ten to life, you would have sworn Debby never heard of Webster Lament Daniels. Eventually as time went by Web got over Debby and did his bid wanting his time to come to make those who shitted on him taste his shit.

"He with his father, he gets him on the weekends." Debby answered avoiding eye contact with Web. She felt uncomfortable talking about her son to Web. She knew she did him wrong by not sticking by him at least as a friend while he was locked up. Especially after the love he showed her when he was home. When Debby started messing around with Ty-Ran at first she felt guilty. The guilt came from the dirty looks she got from people in the projects, especially some of Web's friends but once Ty-Ran laid pipe down and showed her how to get her hustle on with the credit card scams and took her on trips out of town, showering her with expensive gifts, it was a wrap. She took Web's tattooed name off her ankle.

"You like my hair?' Debby asked to change the subject. She removed her scarf showing Web her braids.

"There're nice right? Remember your little girlfriend Deidre from Glenwood Road? Her and her man opened up a beauty salon on the road."

Web remembered Deidre. The pretty light skinned girl who Debby beat up in the bathroom at school. The last time he remembered seeing her was at Shamar funeral. Web went to the funeral with Debby. Debby and Shamar were friends from school, plus Web liked Shamar. Shamar was a cool dude. Deidre was there hugged up with the dark skinned nigga from Linden Plaza. Web remembered the dirty look Deidre gave him and Debby. Maybe I should have messed with her instead of this no good bitch Debby. Deidre probably would have rode the bid with me. Web thought to himself.

"Damn she ain't married the nigga or have kids yet?" Web asked.

Debby shrugged her shoulders. "Liz said Deidre and dude was waiting to get their business up and running before they did all that."

"She is with that?" Web inquired.

"It was her idea. You know the bitch think she all that cause she got degrees and shit. The bitch still holds a grudge against me. Damn bitch, you would think she'd be over it by now. If dude was dicking her right she would of."

Just like you did me bitch! Web thought to himself. All you gotta do is throw a stiff bone and this bitch will run and fetch it.

"So what you going do now that your home? I know you gotta get a job for parole." Debby said.

"I got a job." Web answered sternly. Debby's eyes widened in shock.

"You got a job, where?" As long as Debby knew Web, he never worked an honest day's job in his life. He lived off his favorite craft robbery. No one in their right mind would ever think that Web would work. He would rob the job before he worked there.

"Construction."

Typical, Debby thought to herself. Every guy she knew that come outta jail got a construction job. I guess it was the only job that would quickly hire ex-con. I mean it didn't take a genius to wear an orange flag to direct traffic or pour cement.

As Web was on his way out the door of Debby's apartment, Debby got up in his face. He could smell the cinnamon from the French toast on her breath.

"So will I have access to this anytime I want?" Debby asked grabbing his dick through his pant. Web grinned. Scandalous bitch he thought to himself. Bitch you could have my dick whenever but my heart you will never get close to again.

"Yeah anytime." Web answered with a smile. Debby reached in his pants and massaged his manhood.

"How bout one more round before you bounce," Debby said in a seductive tone. Web obliged. This time he fucked her like he hated her.

As R-Kelly and Usher's song, "The same girl" bumped through the salon mixed in with the buzzing sound of clippers, the clinging sound of scissors and the voices of people, Liz entered the back office where Deidre sat looking at a folder with a small stack of paperwork in it.

"Dee wassup ma. What you doing tonight?" Liz asked playing with one of the long braids that reached her chest. She had two long braids on the side with a part running through the middle of the head. Her Gucci shades added sex appeal to her look.

"Hopefully I'll be done with all this paperwork. If I'd have known running a business would be this back breaking I wouldn't have signed on. All this tax shit is a headache."

"You should go to JRG's with me then relax a little. They say they are having a book release party for that author guy who use to live on 103rd street. That cute boy who lived in Mecca's building." Liz said.

"Who Myles? For real count me in then, that's my boy," Deidre answered excitedly.

"Ain't he still locked up?" Liz asked curiously.

With a sad voice, Deidre answered. "Yeah it's sad too. He all the way in Pennsylvania and didn't get to see his grandmother. They gave him life without parole. He a good dude too."

"Damn bitch you act like you was fucking him or something," Liz joked.

"Your mind is always in the gutter. It wasn't like that at all, he use to always be in our building. He was in love with that dark skinned girl on the first floor."

"Anyway, so it's on?" Liz asked.

"I said yeah hoe. Now let me finish this paperwork."

Liz put up her middle finger before leaving the office. "Hopefully this hoe gets some dick tonight. It's been a while."

Meanwhile across town a man sitting in his black Dodge Magnum answered his cell phone. "Yo"

"A yo son. The nigga real close with his son. The kid is the bait."

"No doubt one."

Chapter 5

Deidre

Everyone showed up dressed to impress at JRG Fashion Cafe on Flatbush Avenue. Most of the people in attendance were friends and family of Myles and his co-author Niko from Queens. Deidre and Liz got out of Deidre's silver Altima looking spectacular. Deidre mint green strapless knee length dress by Donna Karan that accentuated her perfectly curved frame. She was killing 'em with her suede mint green Blahniks. Of course, Liz's clothing was boosted but she was wearing black and gold kimono style silk dress by Versace with black Prada heels. They both wore their hair in cornrows and had expensive shades to add to their fashionable appearance.

The mood in the cafe had a family vibe. It was like a cookout indoors. A lot of people from Bruekelen were there as well as Corona Queens where co-author Niko was from and people from Jamaica Queens, where the author Myles lived for a while.

There were posters of the book called, "Brooklyn Sexy" hung up around the cafe. There was a large photo of Myles on the small stage. It looked like a prison photo. Deidre looked at the picture and saw he was still handsome. He had big waves in his hair. She remembered he had straight pretty hair that made him look like he was Cuban or Dominican. He posed in that all too familiar jail pose bending down.

Deidre and Liz sat at a table for two, a few feet from the stage as a light brown-skinned woman unmistakably Myles sister and a light brown guy walked on the stage towards the microphone.

The light brown skinned guy stepped up to the microphone first. "Good evening ladies and gentlemen my name is Niko I am the co-author of the book "Brooklyn Sexy" along with my brother from another mother, Myles. Before I welcome ya'll to this event, I would like to give ya'll a brief history of my everlasting bond with my co-author and friend, and those who spent a lot of time around him, calls him Dutch.

"I met him in prison in 1999 and from there grew a brotherhood that is unbreakable. I mean if you live in a cell with a guy, a cell no bigger than your bathroom for a year, if ya'll don't wind up killing each other or hating each other then the only thing left is to bond and that's what we did." His statement drew smiles from the crowd. "My love for this guy..." Niko pointed at the photo of Myles then continued. "Grew more when I realized how real he is. He was one out of the many dudes I met in prison that had something productive on his brain other than pictures of naked women, rap videos and sports. Of course, in his predicament, freedom was his foremost objective, but he didn't discourage anyone who was around him. He encouraged me to get my life together and to go out and start my own company and that's what I did. I wish he were here to experience this. That is my dude."

The crowd applauded. Deidre noticed people wiping tears from their eyes. It was a hell of a speech that man gave.

"That Niko is a cutie." Liz whispered in Deidre's ear while she clapped. Deidre just shook her head. Next, the light brown-skinned girl who looked like Myles twin stepped to the mic.

"I don't know what to say after that. Myles is my brother." she chuckled. "I'll say this though..." she paused trying to hold back tears. "If I didn't have my brother I don't know what my life would be like. When my mother passed away, he was the one by my side to help me get through that. My brother and I are tight as a sister and brother could be. Besides my sons, his nephews who love him to death, he is all I have. I hope ya'll enjoy the book."

She walked off the stage not able to hold back the tears. The crowd got silent. A group of family members embraced her as she left the stage. Niko grabbed the microphone.

"That was Alethea Ramzee. Give her a round of applause."

Just as the crowd was applauding, Liz tapped Deidre's knee and mumbled "Dee guess who's here?"

"Who?" Deidre asked nervously.

"Web," Liz mumbled.

"Where?" Deidre asked as if she were on the verge of running. She was anxious to see him. Only to see how he looked after all those years. She heard through the project grapevine that he was muscular and fine as Morris Chestnut. It's not like she wanted to fuck him or be with him. Just curious to see what the man she considered her first boyfriend looked like after years in incarceration. Damn so many of our brothers are in jail. What a shame!

"I wonder who he's here with. Don't niggas get curfews when they on parole?" Liz babbled.

Deidre spotted him standing by himself as he walked out of the men's room. From where he stood wearing a sky blue sleeveless sweater, she noticed how his shoulders look like they were trying to escape from his sweater like a jail break. Oh, God he looks good as hell Deidre told herself.

Her blood pressure went up as he began walking in their direction.

"Damn he's coming this way. Yo that niggas is fiyyine," Liz uttered. Then it seemed as if all the color left Liz face when she noticed Debby and her baby father Ty-Ran come in the cafe.

"Oh shit Dee. Debby and her baby father just walk in this jump off."

"You lying." Deidre snorted.

"My pants on fire if I am, I knew I seen that nigga Maserati on DeKalb."

To make matters worse there was an empty booth next to the seats where Deidre and Liz sat and it looked like Web was headed right to it. He noticed Liz and Deidre as soon as he came over. "Liz, Deidre?" he asked with a look of someone trying to recognize a person.

"Oh shit it is ya'll. What's good ya'll?" Web asked sitting in the empty booth facing towards them. Deidre could smell his cologne and damn it smelled good.

"Web, oh wow it really is you," Deidre said acting surprised.

"Wassup Web? I heard you were home. You look good nigga," Liz muttered. Through his dark skin you could see Web blush.

"Thanks."

"What you doing here?" Deidre asked feeling her hands get sweaty.

"Supporting a Bruekelen dude, it don't matter that he's from the other side, that's old. I'm showing love." Web replied. "Plus his uncle is my man."

"Oh that's right that's black Shameek's nephew." Liz blurted.

"No doubt."

"Oh snap Liz wassup girl." Deidre's whole mood change hearing the unmistakable voice of Debby. Deidre rolled her eyes at Debby but Debby didn't have time to look at Deidre cause her eyes popped out her head when she saw Web.

"Hi Web..." Debby said as if Web was just a guy she knew in passing. "Liz you remember my baby's father Ran right?" Debby said as she and her child's father walked past Web and made a quick stop in front of Liz and Deidre's table.

"Yeah I remember. What's poppin' yo?" Liz greeted.

Ty-Ran gave a quick smile to Liz. His platinum Cuban link necklace with a large diamond flooded Jesus face gave off different colored reflections from the yellow, pink and blue diamonds in it. His watch, an Audemir Piguet also lit up the cafe. He definitely looked like money and had the nerve to be cute in a rough sort of way Deidre thought to herself. He had that Lil Wayne look to him, dreads and all, just a taller version.

When Debby greeted Web all he did was nod his head and didn't look at her or her baby's father. Web played it calm and cool. Deidre thought most likely Web was over Debby and could care less of who she was fucking or having babies with. At least that's what Deidre thought.

Once Debby and Ty-Ran found seats on the opposite side of the cafe far from where Web, Liz and Deidre sat Liz mumbled in Deidre's ear, "Debby looked nervous as hell. She probably peed on herself."

"So Deidre I heard life's been treating you real good salon and all that huh?" Web said changing the tense mood in the atmosphere.

"And where did you hear this?" Deidre asked smiling.

"You know word travels through prison faster than light. We hear about things going on in the streets sometimes people on the street don't hear." Web countered.

"You heard right. Actually me and my boyfriend started the business together."

Web rubbed his chin. "Yeah I heard. That dude we went to school with back in the day. Ya'll still together huh? That's a good thang. I'm happy for you."

Happy? This mufucka broke my heart for this heifer Debby and he gonna sit here and say he's happy for me. If he wants me to be happy now why didn't he want me to be happy then? Deidre thought to herself.

"Thank you," was her only reply.

"Liz what you been up to?" Web asked Liz who was staring at him.

"Nothing. I work at the salon."

"What's the name of the salon?" Web asked.

"D and D's." Deidre answered.

"What's that... oh I know Deidre and what's dudes name?" Web snapped his fingers trying to remember.

"Diondre," Deidre answered.

"Yeah, okay. That's nice."

Deidre was sick of the casual conversation. She wanted to ask him why he hurt her like that. Why did he choose slutty Debby over her? Debby was what Shamar would categorize as Scandals. She couldn't believe herself using one of Shamar's saying like Diondre does but the fact was Debby was a fast ass and if all he wanted was some sex he should of told her instead of leading her on. Deidre never got to talk to Web after that day in the bathroom. Deidre figured after 11 years of being in prison he had more important issues than closing out a teenage relationship. Deidre told herself I guess it was time to let it go. Debby is out of Web's life and so is she. Beating Debby's ass wouldn't be bad though.

"Hey I'm a see ya'll ladies around," Web said as he got up from the booth. His slacks revealed a firm behind. Deidre found herself staring at his ass and caught herself.

"The night is young why you leaving so early?" Liz inquired. Deidre was glad she did cause she wanted to ask the same thing. Deidre liked Web's company. He seemed humble and poised. He seemed to be a very focused man and hopefully it was for the good. God knows how dangerous Web could be.

"I got curfew. Plus I got to go to work in the morning." Web answered expecting the shock look on the girls' faces. He'd been getting that response from everyone he's told that to.

"Job? Where?" Liz asked.

Web smiled. "Construction."

With that, he walked out of the cafe. Liz excused herself to go to the ladies room while the people in the cafe lined up to get autographed books signed by Niko. Deidre dug in her Louis Vutton purse and pulled out fifteen dollars to buy a copy of Brooklyn Sexy.

After shaking Niko's hand as he sat at a table next to Alethea Ramzee she shook Alethea's hand. "I'm from Bruekelen, me and your brother were friends, send, him my love." Deidre said politely. Alethea smiled at Deidre. "I'll do that. In addition, his address is in the back of the book. I know he would be delighted to hear from you and also give him your opinion of the book."

"You know what. I'll do that. Nice meeting

you," Deidre took her copy of the book and walked back to her table. She noticed Liz talking to a tall light-skinned brother by the bar they had seen in the cafe. Deidre gave the guy a look over and noticed the brother was extremely easy on the eyes. In fact, he was drop dead gorgeous once she got a full view of his godly sculpted features. The burgundy turtleneck he wore revealed that he was well built. Not too big and not too small, he was a work of art. His piercing gray eyes, almost cat like sat between chinky features. Deidre thought Boris Kodjoe from Soulfood was the most beautiful man she ever saw until she laid eyes on this brother.

Liz looked over at Deidre and winked her eyes at her. Deidre returned a wink. Deidre hoped Liz didn't play herself and fuck this man tonight, even though Deidre got wet in the panties just looking at him. Knowing Liz, that man will be in that Puerto Rican coochie within the next hour. After talking with the Nubian prince for a half hour, Liz walked over to Deidre.

"Honey that man is so goddamn fine it should be against the law for that," Liz said holding on to Deidre's hand.

"You are not lying. Wow, he is good-looking brother. Where is he from?" Deidre asked.

"He's from right here in Brooklyn Park slope matter fact..." Liz answered waving to him at the bar. "Girl you go on home. I'ma spend some time with Jabbar over there and I'll see you tomorrow."

"Liz I know damn well you ain't...." Deidre mumbled between clenched teeth. Liz placed her hands on her hips and rolled her neck and eyes at Deidre. "Bitch you going home to some dick right now. Can a sister get some too? Damn!"

"Liz you just met him," Deidre scolded.

"I know. I'm going to get to know him better feel me. See ya." Liz walked off leaving Deidre standing there with her jaw touching the floor.

When Deidre got outside of the cafe she saw Debby and her baby father get into his pearl white '07 Maserati and just as Deidre was about to get in her car she noticed Web standing at a phone booth on the corner not talking but looking at Debby and Ty-Ran. When the Maserati pulled off

Web jumped into a parked minivan with someone Deidre couldn't see in the driver's seat. When the Maserati passed the minivan, the minivan pulled off. Deidre shook her head. "Some niggas never change."

Deidre lay in bed that night with Diondre. They just finish a sweat-filled session of lovemaking. Deidre drove home with her panties wet from being in the presence of sexy men like Web and that damn Jabbar. As soon as she got home, she practically raped Diondre.

"Baby you never told me what category you had me in when you and Shamar had ya'll conversation about Brooklyn women." Deidre said laying her head on Diondre dark muscle chest. After telling Diondre about the Debby and Web thang leaving out the part of her and Debby's fight and about her and Web once being an item, Diondre said, "That girl Debby been a scandal since birth."

"And Liz has been a pair of sandals since day one. Don't act shocked by it." Diondre chuckled.

"To be honest baby we didn't know what category to put you in. I mean you're my candle now, but back then we didn't know only because who you hung out with."

"Who Liz?" Deidre lifted her head and asked.

"Not just Liz. What's that girl from Brownsville ya'll use to be in school around? The real nappy headed chick that had those rough ashy hands and use to fight damn near every day. Boy she could fight she was beating dudes up." Diondre reminisced.

"Oh you talkin' bout Shaquana from Tilden. What category was she in?" Deidre inquired.

Diondre sighed before saying. "Don't act like you don't know that girl was stealing out of people lockers, taking coats, school supplies, you name it. She smoked weed like cigarettes. I know she probably got plenty dudes to go around the way to see her and had them robbed if she didn't like the guy. She was a scandal."

"So what that got to do with me?" Deidre continued to inquire.

"You're judged by the company you keep. We didn't have you as a scandal. We were studying you, doing background checks. When we heard you didn't get around, and you weren't a thief that's when I made my move. You've been a candle ever since." Diondre kissed her forehead. Deidre grinned mischievously.

In a sexy seductive voice, she mumbled.

"Right now I wanna be all three categories in bed. I wanna make love to you like a Candle; I want you to fuck me like a Sandal and talk to me dirty like I'm a Scandal."

Deidre slid under the covers and took Diondre's manhood in her warm mouth slurping and moaning as she soaked his shaft with her spit.

Diondre moaned. "Say no mo."

Liz

Liz walked into the salon the next day humming a Keyshia Cole jam with a glow on her face. Deidre walked over to her from putting money in the cash register.

"What you all jolly about nasty ass?" Deidre kidded.

"Don't hate. Ain't nothing like some good loving," Liz said enthused.

"Liz you need to cut it out. Girl what is yo problem?"

"The problem is when it itch somebody gotta scratch it ya dig," Liz laughed.

As she laughed the bass from a candy apple red Chrysler 300's system could be felt as it pulled up in front of the salon. The rims reflected the suns light almost blinding everyone in the shop.

"Damn that whip is banging who is that?" A girl sitting under a blow dryer reading an Essence magazine barked.

"I don't know but whoever the nigga is sure is fine." Another sister added. All the woman and even men in the shop stared as the husky light-skinned brother with a gray Sean John velour suit got out of the Chrysler and walked into the salon.

Deidre looked at the guy and though he looked familiar she couldn't remember where she knew him from. The guy immediately recognized her.

"Wassup Deidre where Dre at?" his voice was smooth.

Deidre put her hand over her mouth in shock. "Oh shit Cornbread?"

"Oh hell no, that ain't Cornbread." Liz roared. Cornbread smiled.

"Liz what up? Where Dre at?"

Deidre got up slowly staring at Cornbread as she went to the back office to get Diondre. Diondre was just walking out the door as Deidre was walking in. She almost bumped into Diondre.

"Oh snap. Dre look who's here," Deidre said like she saw a ghost.

"Who?" Dre asked curiously. Dre immediately recognized Cornbread. Even though the baby fat was gone, the buster brown shoes was gone and the big puffy cheeks that made his eyes look sunk in his face was gone.

"Cornbread. Yo Bread what is the deal man!" Diondre and Cornbread hugged each other and shook hands, as they looked each other up and down. Liz and Deidre were still in shock seeing the chubby kid who wore cheap clothes and tried to be like his stepbrother but couldn't pull it off, turned into a husky and handsome man wearing clothes that weren't cheap, getting out of a nice car and sporting a Breitling watch. He looked like money.

"Dre what's good homey. Damn long time no see."

"I know man. Come on in my office man let's kick it." Dre said as he and Cornbread walked into the office shutting the door behind them.

"Daaamn Cornbread done grew up for real." Liz snorted.

"Who's he?" a girl sitting in a chair waiting to get her hair done asked Liz.

"A nigga me and Dee went to school with. He used to be with Dre back in the day. His brother was Dre's best friend that got killed back then."

"Shit plug a bitch in. Momma needs a new pair of shoes," the girl sang.

"I know that's right," another chimed in.

Deidre shook her head saying to herself, "Scandals and Sandals."

"So Liz what happen with homeboy?" Deidre asked.

"Damn bitch you want my business all out in the streets," Liz snapped. Then she laughed.

"Girl let me tell you. The nigga body is banging. Oh his crib is laced. The nigga got a heart shaped bed, Versace sheets, plush carpeting..."

A girl cut Liz off. "Get to the nasty part Liz we ain't got all day."

"Damn ya'll thirsty. Anyway, the nigga dick ain't all that huge but it's workable. Right before we get it on the nigga tells me he'll be right back. I'm lying in this nigga bed for almost an hour. I damn near fell asleep. I thought he was going to get some chocolate, whip cream, fruits and shit like that. Just as I was about to bounce, he comes in. I'm like what's good nigga? He tells me that he had to run to the phone because his cell phone went dead.

Anyway, we get naked and yo this nigga had me climbing walls just from eating my pussy and my ass. This nigga damn near licked the cheeks off my ass. No lie I came like thirty times. His fuck game is pro and guess what? He wants me to come spend a weekend with him."

"Oooh you go girl!" a customer cheered.

"So how he look?" another girl asked.
Liz inhaled deeply. "Ask Dee." Deidre looked at Liz as if she were asking her an embarrassing question. Deidre looked at the office door.

"He can't hear us Dee. That nigga having a reunion," Liz grunted.

"The brother is so goddamn fine. You'll cum just by staring in his eyes," Deidre said in a hushed tone. The women in the shop hooped and holler at Deidre's revelation.

In the mist of the sexy girl talk Debby walked into the shop looking like she just buried her parents and hadn't slept or bathed since.

"Girl you look a hot mess," Liz said.

In a sad voice that cracked Debby mumbled, "Liz come here I got to talk to you outside."

The look in Debby's puffy eyes made Liz nervous. Even Deidre felt pity for the way Debby looked. She never saw Debby looking sloppy in all the years she knew her. It had to be serious. Then Deidre remembered last night with Debby and her baby's father leaving the Café with Web in tow. Deidre was willing to bet whatever Debby was going through had Web written all over it.

Through the shops window Deidre could see Debby crying while Liz covered her mouth. Liz and Debby hugged and Debby walked off while teary-eyed Liz walked back into the shop. Deidre approached Liz. "Liz what's wrong?"

Liz looked at Deidre with a tear rolling down her face. "Somebody kidnapped Debby's son and left a ransom note on her door."

Chapter 6

Diondre

"I ain't seen you since the funeral man. Where you been what you been up to?" Diondre asked Cornbread as he sat on a leather lounge chair.

"Dog I've been everywhere, the Bronx, Cali, Philly, Baltimore all over the country homey doing my thing."

"Looks like you're doing well for yourself what do you do?" Diondre asked afraid that Cornbread's answer would be what he assumed, being that Cornbread always wanted to be like his stepbrother in all aspects.

"Ah man you know. Got my little weed thang poppin' nothing serious," Cornbread said rubbing his hands together as if he were warming them. Diondre shook his head. "Damn Bread I thought what happen to Shamar would make you realize the streets ain't any good."

"My brother didn't get killed for hustling he got killed by some petty ass stick up niggas," Cornbread said sounding angry.

"I'm sorry they never caught the people responsible," Diondre consoled.

"And what would that have done for anyone it wouldn't have brought Shamar back,"
Cornbread retorted.

Diondre saw that he needed to change the subject; obviously, Cornbread hadn't fully gotten over Shamar's death. How could he, he worshiped the ground he walked on.

"You married, got kids, what's up with your love life?" Diondre asked. Cornbread waved him off. "Nah man ain't married but got a few kids scattered around but no marriage for the kid. That shit for suckers." Diondre laughed. Cornbread sounded just like Shamar.

"How bout you, you ain't marry Deidre yet. Ya'll been together since the Stone Age. Where the ring playboy?"

"Nah not yet. Real soon though," Diondre replied.

"What you ain't find out is she a Candle yet in all these years?" Cornbread asked causing him and Cornbread to howl in laughter.

"Oh naw she definitely a Candle, we just ain't light it up yet." Again more laughter.

"I see Brooklyn did for you what it didn't do for Shamar. You got a successful business running, a good woman, shit Dre life treating you well," Cornbread said seriously.

Cornbread sounded as if he blamed Brooklyn for Shamar's death. Cornbread was born and raised in Brooklyn but Diondre guessed he inherited the dislike for the borough from Shamar. If graduation would have came faster, Shamar wouldn't have been dead on Pitkin Avenue but with the life he was living he probably would of wound up dead on Lenox Avenue right in his Harlem birthplace.

"So what brings you back to BK Cornbread?" Diondre asked.

Cornbread put his head down and shook his head before replying. "My mom passed away. She had breast cancer. My pops ain't taking it too well. So I came to spend some time with the old man.

"Damn I'm sorry to hear that Bread. When's the funeral?"

"Ain't one. My pops cremated her and got the ashes on his nightstand on some other shit.

The nigga buggin' out Dre, he fucked around and got committed to Bellevue," Cornbread said sadly.

"Nah Bread. He'll get over it just give him some time," Diondre consoled.

"Nigga she been dead for two years now."

Cornbread left the shop promising Dre that he would stop by often so they could hang out like old times. Though he travels in and out of state often, Cornbread informed Dre that he lived in the Bronx when he was in New York and the Bronx wasn't that far away. Dre told Cornbread that when they start doing hair shows out of state if it was a state Cornbread frequented they would hangout then. Cornbread made a promise to do so.

"Hay Bread...!" Dre called out to Cornbread before he got in his Chrysler.

"There's always love for you in Brooklyn. Remember that."

"What's wrong baby girl? Where you at cause you sure ain't here in this restaurant with me." Jabbar dressed casually in a short sleeve polo shirt and slacks said as he and Liz sat in a restaurant named Las Trinas situated in the bottom floor of a Brownstone in Fort Greene.

"I'm sorry, it's not you, it's something that I can't talk about," Liz answered while picking at her shrimp scampi with her fork not eating.

"If you can't talk about what's bothering you to a friend then who can you talk too?"

Jabbar said with a voice and tone that made Liz feel comforted. She wanted to talk to someone about it hoping that someone could come up with a solution before something went terribly wrong, but what could anyone do.

"One of my friend's son got kidnapped and she has no idea who did it. They left a ransom note for a hundred G's. She doesn't have a hundred G's," Liz said as if she were pleading with Jabbar for help. Help to understand why. Why would someone do that to a child? An innocent child?

"Who's the kid's father? Maybe they or whoever did it thinks he's got that type of money," Jabbar commented.

"I mean most likely he does but why not kidnap him or run up in his spot?"

Jabbar shrugged his shoulders. "Baby I'm not a street cat so I don't know what motivates people to do treacherous things like that. But it sounds like someone or persons know that the father is close with his son and is using that as a sure way to get what they want."

"Maybe you're right. I just hope they don't hurt that poor boy. He's got a bright future ahead of him."

Jabbar held Liz's hand across the table. "I don't think that will happen. This ain't the 80's. That kid will be aight."

After dinner and a movie, Liz went with Jabbar back to his place for a nightcap. They sat on his tan leather couch drinking an expensive bottle of Ace of Spades. Jabbar stared into Liz's eyes as she drank. The beauty of his face and eyes hypnotized Liz. Where have you been all my life? Liz asked herself. Jabbar kissed her gently on her soft sensual lips. He grabbed the drink out of her hand and placed it on a glass coffee table.

He sucked lightly on her bottom lip down to her neck. Liz moaned as the warmth of his lips sent erotic sensations through her body. He slipped the spaghetti straps of her dress down off her shoulders. She pulled the dress down revealing her firm breasts with nipples hard as tire caps.

Jabbar squeezed her nipples gently causing Liz to inhale deeply. He placed his mouth on her nipples and sucked her into ecstasy.

Jabbar lifted Liz's body and carried her to his bed. He laid her down on her back as he kissed her passionately. She reached for the bottom of his pants and quickly got his pants down.

He kicked his pants off while Liz pulled his boxers down. She stroked his manhood while he kissed her and pulled her skirt to her waist. She released his hard pole to pull her skirt off. Jabbar slid her thong to the side as he placed his middle finger in her cave while using his thumb to play with her clit. Liz arched her back and moaned.

"Jabbar I want you to make love to me," Liz mumbled. She couldn't believe she said those words. Liz usually wanted a guy to fuck her brains out until they both were worn out. She barely found a man who was gentle and made her feel wanted. Jabbar did that.

Jabbar kissed his way down to her belly button eventually reaching her spot. While he sucked and licked her clit his finger found her G-spot.

"Jabbar! Jabbar! Jabbar! Oh God, please don't stop. God that feel so good!" she grunted.

Jabbar hand became drenched in her juices. When the feeling became too much for Liz to handle she positioned her body in a sixty-nine position and took Jabbar in her mouth. She soaked him with spit and moaned while rubbing his manhood against the walls of her mouth and on her face.

Jabbar moaned as Liz played with his balls while giving him some of the best head he'd had in a while. With her ass and pussy in his face Jabbar licked her clit then slid his tongue to her asshole. Liz almost lost her breath as his tongue massage her shit box.

She moaned and orgasm on Jabbar's face as he took her and her juices in his mouth.

Liz then straddled Jabbar's manhood with her ass facing him. He squeezed her soft cheeks then spread them watching his manhood soaked in her cream go in and out of her fat love nest. Her shaved private turned Jabbar on. Jabbar watched as she flexed her stuff making it grip his stiffness causing him to groan, "Oh shit this some good stuff girl. Damn ma!"

He placed Liz in doggy style, her favorite position. As he hit it from the back he slapped her cream colored ass and that's when the Spanish came out. "Ooooh Poppy right there poppy fuck this chocha. Oooh fuck poppy!" She looked back at Jabbar as he pumped and the Spanish did it to him cause he felt himself about to explode.

"Oh shit! Oh shit! Yeah! Yeah! Oh yeah," he roared as he exploded on her ass watching her rub it on herself then lick her fingers.

Afterwards, the couple lay in each other's arms. Liz leaned her head on his chest rubbing his six-packed stomach while listening to his heart beat. She imaged his heart beating her name.

She pictured him on one knee proposing to her on the Brooklyn waterfront facing the Manhattan skyline. She fell asleep in his arms with a smile on her face. Liz was finally in love.

Chapter 7

Debra

"This nigga ain't in his son's life like that. The only time he plays daddy is when he wants to fuck or his mom want to see lil Ty-Ran. He might not even pay the ransom." Debby sat on the couch crying to Liz about the kidnapping of her son.

"What did he say when you told him?" Liz inquired. Debby sucked her teeth. "The nigga tried to flip it on me talkin' bout if I was at the school before they let out this wouldn't of happen. Shit I ain't tryna hear that because that ain't goin to get my son back."

"Did you call the cops?" Liz asked, receiving a look from Debby that said 'please.'

"The note said if the police get involved they're goin kill my baby," Debby began to sob. Liz hugged her.

"Debby its going be aiight ma. Ty-Ran will be home. What did his father say about paying the ransom?" Liz asked.

"He said he'll look into it. That ain't the type of money that he could just get up in a day.

He was talking like he doesn't give a fuck!" Debby barked.

"What about Web do you think he'll help?" Liz didn't know why she asked that question knowing their history and how Debby left the man while he was doing time. She just didn't know what else to say.

"Hell fucking no I ain't ask that nigga. That grimy nigga probably got something to do with it. You know how he gets down. He came here the other day asking bout my son and his father. I swear Liz if that nigga hurt my son. I'll walk right over to Williams Avenue and choke his old grandmother to death."

"When and where do they want the money?" Liz asked.

"The note said to drop it off under the L train on Livonia Avenue by Friday." It was Tuesday.

After Liz left Debby's house, Debby stared at the ransom note crying when her doorbell rang. She got up and looked out her peephole. Her blood boiled as she saw Web on the other side of the door. Debby leaned on the door crying. "Web I'm sorry I hurt you. I never did a bid with a man. I was young and dumb but please don't take it out on my son!" Debby cried.

Web got close to the door and mumbled. "Debby you trippin ma. I would never do anything to nobody's kids. That's not my style and never been my style. Open the door baby let me see if I could help."

He sounded convincing to Debby and as she thought about it. Web has never involved innocent people in his doings. Web was an old school gangsta.

"Debby listen ma. I'm not holding a grudge

BROOKLYN SEXY PART 1

for that. I had been over that. I'm not tryna rob no more, I'm tryna chill. I'm too old for the bullshit." With that said, Debby opened the door. She believed him or at least she wanted to.

She hugged Web and sobbed. "Web I'm sorry I just want my baby back."

"I'ma look into it Deb. I know a lot of people, trust me on this," Debby looked Web in his eyes and saw genuine concern. She kissed him on the lips. "Web I swear I regret hurting you please forgive me."

"I been forgave you. I wouldn't be here if I didn't." Web lied.

On the other side of Flatlands Avenue Ty-Ran and a friend from his Red Hook neighborhood watches Web walked out of Debby's apartment. Ty-Ran rented a gray Nissan Sentra just in case Debby was looking around. She wouldn't notice him in a car that wasn't his.

"I'm telling you son that bitch up to something. She probably staged this whole thing for a nigga. That might be the nigga there," Ty-Ran's homey said as they sat low with their seats reclined.

"We goin' find out who duke is. If that bitch tryna get me we goin lose her and him." Ty-Ran pulled off.

***

"Deidre, Dre, this is my friend Jabbar. Jabbar these are my best friends and employers."

Liz introduced Jabbar as they gathered in Diondre's office. Jabbar immediately smelled the aroma of incense burning as he entered the nicely decorated office. Wall to wall carpeting, a book shelf stocked with black history books and portrait size posters of historical black figures, like Malcolm X, Elijah Mohammad, Dr. King and Minister Farrakhan, the office was immaculate. Diondre sat behind the desk in a leather recliner Deidre sat on a lounge chair.

Diondre stood to shake Jabbar's hand; afterwards Jabbar greeted Deidre with a kiss on her hand. Deidre felt a tingle between her legs and her blood went up a few degrees. Seeing Jabbar up close Deidre had to compose herself when he kissed her hand, she felt the softness of his lips and the firmness of his hands. His eyes told her he was gentle yet sheer masculinity could be sensed from there. Dam he is all that. I have to get away from him before Diondre catches me staring, Deidre told herself.

"It is nice to meet ya'll. Liz told me so much about ya'll, indeed you're a handsome couple," Jabbar complimented looking at Diondre and Deidre.

"I have to run to the store," Deidre said tripping on her way out the office.

"It's good to meet you also brother. You must be special because Liz has never introduced me to a boyfriend," Diondre said.

"Boy shut up!" Liz said laughing.

"I'm flattered." Jabbar said smiling at Liz.

"So where are you from and what do you do?" Diondre asked like a concerned father.

Even though Diondre felt Liz was a sandal.

He grew to really care about her. He noticed how much Liz cared and loved Deidre and to him that meant a lot. Liz was a cool chick to be around; she was humorous, pretty and brutally honest. Diondre knew that once she met the right man she would make that man happy.

Jabbar told Diondre about his Park Slope upbringing and his job as a financial consultant.

"A financial consultant, so you know a thing about money?" Diondre inquired.

"If I didn't meet Liz, money would be my only love," Jabbar said jokingly.

Diondre liked Jabbar's vibe. He was a cool, smooth, articulate brother like himself. He came from a two-parent home that instilled in him good morals and values, the same way Diondre was raised. The only disagreement Diondre had with his Baptist parents was leaving Brooklyn. Diondre's parents retired and moved to Florida to live the rest of their days away from the cold New York winters and the vicious, unforgiving streets of Brooklyn. Diondre called them every weekend to see how they were doing. Last time he spoke to his parents they were in Africa doing charity work with the likes of Danny Glover and Oprah Winfrey. As with his sisters, he saw them at family reunions. They had busy lives.

"So if I need some advice I can come to you? Are your consulting fees reasonable?" Diondre asked.

"Very. Being that your damn near family to Liz I don't have a problem giving free consultation,"

Jabbar said.

"Do ya'll want me to help plan the wedding?" Diondre joked causing Jabbar and Liz to howl in laughter. "By the way how old are you?" Diondre asked.

"Thirty-five."

After promising Diondre to visit him and help him with some future business plans Jabbar walked out of the office with Liz in tow holding on to his arm. The women in the shop gawked and stared at Jabbar with jaws on the floor. Liz looked at their faces and grinned. "He's mines bitches pick ya'll faces up!" Liz licked her tongue at them as she walked out the door.

"Ask him do he have brothers. Shit even a son will do. I want those genes up in me," a girl snickered as Liz walked out of the shop.

"I'm telling you Debby if some nigga you fucking is behind this I'm coming for both of ya'll."

"I can't believe you'd think I'd do that to my own son. If I wanted to set yo ass up I could of did it letting a mufucka know where you live or when you coming here to put yo dick in me.

Fuck you Ran!" Debby cried into her cell phone while pacing in her living room. Ever since the kidnapping, she only left her house once. She didn't shower, damn near hasn't eaten since. She ignored the smell coming from her under arms and body. All she thought about was the safe return of her son. God she missed him. She stared at his pictures. She slept in his bed and cried herself to sleep. She was a mess and Ty-Ran accusing her of being part of the plot was making things worst.

"I got half the money. Why don't you ask your boosting buddies or your boyfriends to help with the rest," Ty-Ran said harshly.

"Don't you think I asked my friends? Mufuckas can't just pop up with that kind of money Ran," Debby lied. She didn't have the nerve to ask any of her boosting friends for money. She lived her life wanting her friends to think that she was well off. Like she didn't need to boost and scam anymore fronting like she had money put up. The reality was Debby spent money faster than she made it mostly on her son.

"You got to come up with something. We only got 3 days left," Ty-Ran said then hung up. Debby slammed the phone down on the couch, sat down and sobbed with her face in her hand.

***

Later that night Liz invited Jabbar over to her apartment. They watched a movie after Liz cooked them a dinner consisting of fried fish and rice, which they washed down with some wine that Jabbar bought. They sat on the couch and talked. Liz heard a knock at her door. *Somebody is about to ruin the mood up in here, Liz* thought as she walked to the door. When she saw through the peephole that it was Debby she quickly answered. "Deb wassup ma you aight?"

With the same sad look she had since the kidnapping Debby said, "Liz I need to talk to you."

"Come in, sit down. Jabbar this is my friend Debby. Debby this is Jabbar," Debby waved while Jabbar said hello.

"Do you want me to comeback Liz I didn't mean to mess up anything," Debby said sniffing.

"Of course not Debby," Liz lied. "Tell me what's up ma."

Wiping her eyes with toilet paper Debby explained that Ty-Ran had half the ransom and wanted her to come up with the rest. He told me to ask my friends.

"Liz they're gonna kill my baby if I don't get this money up," Debby sobbed.

Liz hugged Debby. "Debby no they're not, I'm gonna talk to Diondre and Deidre. I'll ask them to loan me the money and I'll work it off at the salon."

Debby hugged Liz real tight. "Liz I love you ma I swear. Thank you so much," Debby cried on Liz shoulders.

"Now listen Debby I'm not sure they'll do it but I'll try my hardest. If not you gotta try to buy sometime and I can scrape up as much as I can, if I gotta go downtown to Macy's and walk out with half the store I will aight."

Jabbar sat and listened to the two women talking about the kidnap for ransom Liz had told him about. His respect and admiration for Liz shot up to its max. She was a real friend. A dude needed a woman like that on his side. He wished he could help but his money was wrapped up in a lot of investments as they spoke.

"I'll call you tomorrow morning after I talk to

them," Liz promised. Debby walked out of Liz apartment feeling a little relieved. Not fully cause she still didn't have her son.

That night Jabbar made love to Liz as if it was their first and last time together. In the mist of the sweat-drenched love making Jabbar whispered in her ear. "Liz I'm falling in love with you."

Liz replied, "Me too poppy. Now shut up and fuck this pussy."

Chapter 8

Diondre

Liz thought it would be better if Debby came with her to talk to Diondre and Deidre. Once they got a look at how Debby looked, they would probably be more sympathetic to her plight. At first Debby thought it was a bad idea. "You know Deidre hates my guts ain't no way in the world that's gonna work."

"Debby if I go in there without you the first thing they goin think is that you running a scam on all of us." Liz shot back. Debby knew Liz was right so she agreed to go with Liz.

Diondre and Deidre were in the office when Liz walked in with Debby in tow. When Deidre saw Debby, her eyes widened in shock and she shot a look of confusion at Liz.

"Dee, Dre I have something very important to ask ya'll. I just need ya'll to hear us out," Liz said humbly.

Liz began to relay the story to Diondre and Deidre, and then Debby cut in telling the whole thing while sobbing in between. Deidre didn't want to reveal her feelings towards Debby because she hid that part of her life from Diondre, but surprisingly she believed Debby. Debby looked a mess. Her face was thinning and she was in need of a shower and makeover.

Diondre asked Debby to wait outside the office he wanted to speak to Liz in private.

Debby knew coming to them was a bad idea. She excused herself. Just as Diondre was about to resume speaking Cornbread came out of the office bathroom.

"Damn man you been in there so long I forgot you was here," Diondre said. Cornbread rubbed his belly. "I ate something that ran through me."

"Uh uh no you didn't Bread," Deidre spat in disbelief that he would do number two in the office.

"Hey man nature hit me on the hip."

"Hey cornbread," Liz greeted.

"What's good Liz. Hey, I couldn't help but overhear ya'll conversation. That's Debby with the big butt use to go to Jeff out there?" Cornbread asked.

"Yeah that's her," Deidre said.

"Ah man Liz, call her in here. That's my homey," Cornbread snorted. Everyone in the office looked confused.

"Homey since when?" Diondre asked shockingly.

"Since back in the day she used to always be at the crib."

Everyone in the office said in unison "Shamar." Cornbread shrugged his shoulders. "Yeah he was tapping that but she was real cool with my family. I know her baby father too, Ran from Red Hook. He spend money with some people of mines. If he said he got half, then that's what he got."

Liz ran and got Debby. When Debby walked in Cornbread smiled at her. At first, she didn't recognize him then as she stared she remembered the face.

"Cornbread oh shit boy wassup?" Debby and Cornbread hugged.

"Damn Deb you aight? You look tore up. Listen I heard what happen. I was in the bathroom when ya'll was kickin it. You know we like family and Ran is people. So come take a ride with me and I'll get you that paper."

Debby's face lit up like the fourth of July.

"You will? Oh, thank you so much Bread. You don't know how much this means to me. Thank you!" Debby jumped into Cornbread arms and hugged him.

"Before we do that, you need to shower and geta hair do." Cornbread said causing everyone to laugh including Debby.

Cornbread knew Debby could be shady but he remembered how much she liked Shamar and how nice she was to his mother. Even though Shamar didn't like her as much as she did him, Debby eventually got the picture, she still paid respects to him by coming to the funeral with her new boyfriend Web.

As Cornbread and Debby drove to get the money Debby stared at him telling herself that Cornbread was totally different from when they were in high school. He didn't get a lot of girls cause the way he dressed and how chubby he was and Debby use to feel sorry for him. So she treated him like a little brother. Cornbread had a crush on her. Now Debby realized that Cornbread was cute and any woman would want him as a man now. If the girls in high school didn't look his way then if they could see him now boy would they piss themselves.

They reminisced about the old days, they laughed and Debby even cried when she heard about the death of Cornbread's mother. "She was the sweetest lady in the world. I really miss her and your brother," Debby consoled.

After Cornbread picked up the money he placed it a Nike shoe box and placed the box in a plastic bag, he drove Debby home.

"When all this is over with, call me we'll hang-out sometimes," Cornbread said walking Debby to her door.

"You don't want to come in?" Debby asked.

Cornbread hugged her. "Nah I gotta run but like I said call me."

Debby promised that she would and as soon as she got her son back she told herself she would.

***

The next morning the money was placed under the L train on Livonia Avenue. A man sitting parked in a black rented Nissan Maxima a block away from the drop off point dialed a number on his cell phone. "The drop was made."

"Anybody knows where the other half came from?" the voice on the line asked.

"Her friends that own the salon on Glenwood Road." The phone clicked off.

Debby couldn't sleep the whole night after the money was dropped off. She sat in her living room staring out the window waiting for her son to be brought home. She couldn't have been happier when she saw big Ty-Ran's midnight blue four door 600 Benz pull up and her son got out of the car running towards the house.

"My baby oh god come here baby!" Debby yelled running outside taking hold of her son. She hugged him like she would never let go. She vowed that he would never leave her sight again. If she had too, she would sit in his classes at school with him. One thing was for sure, she told herself she was getting out of Brooklyn.

Big Ty-ran gave Debby a look of pity. "Hey Deb I'm sorry I accused you. You know how shit could be."

Debby rolled her eyes. "No, I don't know how shit could be Ran. Tell me about it." With that said, she walked in the house with her son in her arms.

Ty-Ran got back in the Benz where one of his homies sat in the back. "Yo get in the front son," Ty-Ran ordered. The homey did as he was told.

When Ty-Ran began driving, his homey said." Yo, son I found out who dude is. They call the nigga Web. The nigga old school nigga be juxing mad shit. He's the nigga that robbed the rap nigga with Mut and The Dominican in Times Square. He just came home. My son Pit told me dude was a homo when they were locked up in the mountains together but he definitely behind this shit. Even though your BM was fucking dude I don't think she was in on it."

Ty-Ran nodded his head. "It's time to wash this nigga up then."

***

Deidre had to stop herself from staring across the table as her, Diondre, Liz and Jabbar double dated at a restaurant called Zilo's in lower Manhattan. The candle on the table reflected off Jabbar's gray eyes making him look even sexier as the candle light made his smooth skin glow.

They all sat and listened as he spoke of his ex-girlfriend of four years who broke his heart by leaving him for a correction officer that worked on Riker's Island. *Either that correction officer was God himself or that bitch done lost her mind,* Deidre thought to herself. The way Jabbar told the story he made you want to reach out and hug him.

That's exactly what Liz did. "You got me now baby. I'm not going anywhere."

Jabbar gave her a peck on the lips. "I know, you betta not."

"Wasn't that nice of Cornbread to give the money to Debby?" Deidre asked changing the subject. Hearing Jabbar's broken heart story was making her sad.

"No doubt," Liz blurted.

"That was a good look. For real for real she looked so sad I was just about to cough up the money," Diondre said.

"You're so sweet honey," Deidre said kissing

Dre on his lips.

Sipping on his wine Jabbar looked confused. "Who's Cornbread?"

Diondre told Jabbar who Cornbread was. Diondre reminisced about growing up with Shamar and Cornbread then relayed the story about Cornbread hearing Liz and Debby's plea for help while he took a dump in the office bathroom of the salon and giving Debby the money.

"Even though his food didn't agree with him I bet you Debby agreed with that food that caused him to have the runs," Jabbar joked making them all laugh. Jabbar and Deidre locked eyes and Jabbar could read the look. It was a look of a woman who liked what she saw. Jabbar smiled. Jabbar wasn't the only one that caught the look. Liz did also and she didn't like it. By the end of the night, Diondre felt he found himself a genuine friend in Jabbar. A male companion he's been without since Shamar's death and Cornbread disappearance from Brooklyn. Unlike Shamar, Jabbar was able to speak on many different topics and what impressed Diondre even more was Jabbar's knowledge of black history and his opinion of the conditions of black people today.

"I love our people. It's just sad that we don't love each other. I mean look at how the people acted when the cops shot that boy in Queens fifty-one times. Everyone was upset and took to the streets. I mean that was a sad and tragic event but I know a guy on my old block in Park Slope who got shot that many times by another guy from the block, and nobody took to the streets about that. That boy went to jail did his time came home and they had a cookout for him on the block when he got out. What message does that send to our children?" Jabbar preached. Everyone at the table nodded in agreement. Deidre thought he was adorable.

That night when Deidre and Diondre got home, Deidre once again damn near raped him.

'What's gotten into you lately baby?" You've been real freaky?" Diondre said trying to catch his breath after about an hour of lovemaking.

"What, I can't freak off with my man?" Deidre asked looking up at the ceiling feeling guilty about picturing Jabbar making love to her while in bed with Diondre.

"Oh I'm not complaining I'm just wondering where it's coming from."

Deidre rubbed his chest. "You turn me on something fierce." Deidre spoke seductively. She reached under the sheet and stroked his semi erect organ. When she felt him bone up in her hands, she smiled. "Round three, ding!"

That next morning before going to work Liz dropped by to see Debby. When Debby answered the door Liz smiled to see that Debby she knew was back. Her hair was done, her skin glowed and she smelled good.

"Hey Debby wassup ma?" Liz greet jovially.

"Nothing baby wassup?" Debby hugged Liz inviting her in.

"Where's my boy" Liz asked.

"He's in his room sleeping. I'm not letting him go to school for a little while. I'm a let him rest a little, he been through a lot." Debby said.

"I know what you mean," Liz agreed.

Now Debby noticed a worried look on Liz face and she knew Liz had something on her mind she wanted to get off.

"Liz you look like something's bothering you. I'm your girl for life you know you can talk to me about anything." Debby said comfortingly.

"Yeah I know. It's just I don't wanna jump to conclusions. But my gut is telling me I'm right," Liz said in a sullen voice.

"What is it?" Debby asked concerned.

"I think Deidre likes my man." Ever since Liz saw that look in Deidre's eyes, she knew Deidre wanted Jabbar. Liz remembered the look in Deidre's eyes when she started seeing Diondre. Debby asked Liz how did she figure and Liz explained the look she gives Jabbar.

"I'm saying Liz a lot of women look at him like that. The nigga is fine as hell. That don't mean she's going to fuck him. Don't get all insecure now, that ain't even you." Debby said.

"Am I being insecure?" Liz asked as if she was embarrassed at herself.

"I'm saying you know the bitch better than I do and I wouldn't put nothing pass her. Ya'll let that goody-two shoes act fool ya'll not me. There some dirt in that bitch closet with bones buried under it but this your first time in love so you are paranoid. That love shit ain't no joke Liz. Don't let it get to you like that. Cause the pain of a broken heart is a mufucka."

"You right. I just needed to talk to somebody, " Liz said cheering up a little.

"Shit if it was me I would have asked that bitch what the fuck is you looking at him like that for. You know I whooped that bitch ass before and I'll do it again."

"So what you been up to?" Liz asked getting off the topic. Even though she was having bad thoughts about Deidre wanting her man, she still was Deidre's best friend. Liz loved Deidre a lot and she realized she shouldn't let a man or no one come between that.

"Oh yeah I got some shit I want you to look at," Debby disappeared into her room for a few minutes and then when she emerged she was holding a bunch of bags and clothes with the tags still on them.

"Damn Deb you ain't waste no time, Liz grumbled.

"You know it. My son got to eat and sitting on my ass won't feed him. I got everything Chanel, some shit I can't pronounce, Prada, Paper Demin, Seven Roca-Wear, Citizens of Humanity name it it's here." Debby tossed the clothes on her couch and pick through them showing Liz.

"Oooh wassup with this Tru Religion jump off?" Liz said holding the expensive jeans to her body.

"They're your size too. Go ahead they're yours. And whatever else you want take it," Debby said.

"What ya'll having a party?"Liz heard a voice

say when she looked to see who the voice belong to she was shocked. There in a pair of large silk Versace underwear with a large platinum chain with a medallion resting near his potbelly was Cornbread. Liz looked at Debby with a devilish grin. Debby blushed embarrassingly.

***

When Liz got to work that morning, she smiled at Deidra without saying a word. "Liz wassup girl?" Deidre greeted.

Liz nodded while walking to her chair to get her stuff ready for her first appointment. Deidre sensed a little attitude in Liz demeanor but brushed if off as maybe it was that time of the month for Liz. You know how that time makes a woman get. Then Deidre became confused when Diondre opened his office door and called Liz. "Liz I need to holler at you."

"Hey Dre wassup baby I'll be right there, "Liz said as if she was happy to see him.

"Liz, I left Jabbar's card in my crib I need his number real quick. We got this investment plan and I need to holla at him now." Diondre said as Liz stepped in his office.

Liz removed her cell phone from her hip. "I got the number right here in my phone," Liz said looking through her list of numbers on her phone.

"Here it is." Liz read off the numbers while Diondre put it in his phone.

"Thanks Liz."

"Anytime Dre." Liz said walking off. Then she turned back into Dre's office. "Dre guess who I just saw at Debby house all in his drawers?"

"Who?" Dre asked curiously.

"Between me and you...... Liz whispered conspiratorially. "Cornbread."

"Get outta here!" Dre roared while laughing.

"Ssh Dre," Liz mumbled looking out of the salon with her body half way in the office holding the door. Liz noticed Deidre looking at them with a questionable look.

"That girl is crazy. I'm glad I didn't cough up the money now. She probably would have knocked on my door with a trench coat on with nothing under it." Dre joked.

"You ain't shit, Liz said letting the door closed.

Liz glanced at Deidre giving her a half smile as she put on her pink over coat that had her name in script on the upper corner and opposite side of the coat the words D and D's. Liz spotted one of her customers entering the salon.

"Keisha what's good girl?" Liz smiled from ear to ear.

Deidre told herself she was going to have a talk with Liz later on. She didn't know what's her problem was but she was going to get to the bottom of it today.

Chapter 9

Debra

"Liz just had to open her mouth huh?" Cornbread asked Diondre while they ate a Sunday brunch at Cornbread's northeast Bronx apartment in Co-op city.

"Yeah you know how women are, they can't hold water that's why when they can't hold a baby no longer they say their water broke," Diondre joked. He informed Cornbread about Liz's revelation about Cornbread creeping with Debby.

"I can't front Dre I always had a crush on her plus that ass," Cornbread shook his head with his eyes closed picturing Debby's large dark chocolate rump.

"Yeah the sister is packing heavy I'll admit but don't let your feelings get ahead of you," Diondre warned. Diondre heard through the grapevine that Debby's love nest done whipped the most macho acting gangstas in Brooklyn and got their hearts crushed.

"C'mon Dre my brother's words and spirit still linger with me. No disrespect but falling in love with a Brooklyn chick is a no-no in my book. To me they still just sandals and scandals."

Cornbread stuck by that motto he heard many of times from Shamar. "Don't get me wrong though, there are some sexy chicks in Brooklyn. I love the rough edginess that they give off. I find their attitudes a turn on but wifing one of them? Not!"

Diondre shook his head. He just didn't get it. How could you judge a whole borough of women by the actions of a few? Diondre has yet to be a victim of these scandalous, trifling chicks that Shamar, Cornbread and the other men attribute to Brooklyn women. Many times prejudice comes from men who are from Brooklyn themselves. Diondre has met men from the other boroughs of New York who don't share those views about sisters from the County of Kings.

A guy he knew from Manhattan once expressed to him; "You don't have to have a Benz and have a lot of money to please a Brooklyn girl. All you have to do is be a real cat and she will be with you. That's why I love me some Brooklyn girls."

"Debby is a cool chick and that's just it. We're friends who fuck each other. I mean can you blame her?" Cornbread patted himself on the back.

Diondre giggled. "Oh you really big on yourself!"

After brunch, Cornbread and Diondre drove to a bowling alley in White Plains. Diondre asked Cornbread to stop at a corner Bodega so he could purchase a newspaper. When Diondre walked in the store, he was surprised to see Jabbar in the store with a gallon of milk in his hand wearing a tank top, sweat pants and leather sandals. "Jabbar yo what's up man?" Diondre said enthused.

Jabbar looked as if he saw a ghost or as if he was busted for stealing something. "Dre what's up man what you doing up here?" Jabbar asked sounding nervous.

"I'm up here with a friend. Matter fact my boy Cornbread I was telling you about he's right outside. What you gotta crib up here too. You look like you just woke up?" Diondre asked skeptically wondering if Jabbar was there creeping with another chick. His nervous demeanor made Diondre suspicious of that.

"Nah Dre my cousin Will live up here. He just came back from Iraq and the family is spending a weekend with him," Jabbar answered looking at the milk avoiding eye contact with Dre.

A sign of a man lying, Dre thought.

Dre stepped close to Jabbar's face and mumbled. "Jabbar Liz is in love with you, don't hurt her please. She doesn't deserve that. I never saw her this happy and trust me she has lived a life that the average person would of killed themselves over. Do right by her. Don't worry I won't snitch you out, just be real that's all I ask."

"Dre I'm telling you the truth. I wouldn't hurt Liz. My cousin just got back from the war," Jabbar said looking Dre in his eyes.

"Aight man. Listen we gotta get together.

That plan will make us rich so let's do this," Diondre said as he grabbed the paper, paid the clerk and walked out the store.

"No doubt," Jabbar said then exhaled as Dre disappeared. Diondre and Cornbread spent about an hour and a half bowling. Afterwards Cornbread drove Dre to his car in a Co-op city parking garage.

"Dre I'll call you tomorrow. In fact, I'll stop by. I'm gonna be in Brooklyn tomorrow," Cornbread yelled to Dre as they had their cars parallel to each other.

"For what Debby?" Dre asked sarcastically.

"Nah nigga I gotta pick up some money. I'll holla. You got jokes too," Cornbread said then pulled off as the wheels of his Chrysler screeched making Dre's skin crawl.

When Cornbread opened his apartment door and stepped in to turn the light on, he never got a chance to hit the switch. For a split second, he felt something hard hit him on the back of his head and lights out.

***

Debby coughed as the potent weed smoke rushed her lungs. Her eyes watered as she passed the blunt with one hand, while holding a sheet over her breast. Ty-Ran grabbed the blunt after looking at his watch.

Debby reached under the sheet and gently stroked his manhood making blood quickly rush to his organ making it erect. Once hard to her satisfaction, she placed her head under the sheets and wrapped her lips around his shaft. She tasted her own juices as she deep throated him without gagging on his long pole. Ty-Ran rested his head on the headboard and grabbed her head as she moved it up and down and round in a circular motion.

Ty-Ran moaned as Debby teased the tip of his member with her tongue while massaging his balls with her hand. Within five minutes from her toe curling, head giving performance Ty-Ran was releasing his babies down Debby's throat. She didn't let one drop fall on her bed or back on Ty-Ran.

While Ty-Ran was getting dressed he looked at Debby skeptically "Why you looking at me like that?" Debby asked blowing smoke in the direction of the ceiling.

"Who's Web?" Ty-Ran asked. Debby's heart went from zero to sixty in a split second.

"Who?" Debby asked picking up the ashtray and clipping the blunt avoiding Ty-Ran's gaze.

"Don't act stupid Deb. You heard me who the fuck is Web?" Ty-Ran barked angrily.

Why is he bringing this nigga Web up? And who the fuck told him about Web? Probably some hating ass bitch tryna make my baby father her man.

"He's from around my way why you asking about Web?" Debby said trying to not sound nervous.

"You use to fuck with him and you still fucking him right?"

"I used to fuck with him back in the day way before I met you. And no I'm not fucking." Debby lied. She tried to convince herself she was telling the truth because she hasn't had sex with him ever since her son's kidnapping.

"You know what Debby? That's why we can't be together because you a lying ass bitch."Ty-Ran said walking out of her room.

Debby quickly jumped up out of her bed. She grabbed her silk kimono and caught up to Ty-Ran.

"Ty-Ran, Ty-Ran!" she yelled grabbing his arm.

"Debby get the fuck off me!" Ty-Ran commanded.

"Wait. Listen to me I have nothing to do with him. Since he's been home he stopped by a couple of times to talk but that's it. We're just friends. I left him for you." Debby pleaded.

"Nah Deb. You got with me because dude got locked up. You ain't ride with the nigga. I know if I go away, you won't ride with me. You're trifling."

"That's not true. You're my son's father so if God forbid you go away I'll have no choice but to be there for you. Not just for me but for our son. Web means nothing to me Ran I swear." Debby pleaded her heart out.

"Oh I know that for sho. And you know why I know because that nigga is the one who kidnapped our son. So if you don't give a fuck about dude stay away from him. He ain't gonna be around long any way."

Debby felt like she was about to vomit. "How do you know that?" Debby asked.

"I know a lot of people Deb. Nigga know me and respect me in these streets. I know all about that gay booty bandit nigga. If you fucked the nigga since he been home you betta go get yo self checked cause he was running up in niggas in jail like a marathon runner."

Debby vomited on her leather couch as Ty-Ran walked out of her apartment. When Debby got herself together, she dialed Cornbread's number on her cell phone.

His voice mail came on. "Cornbread I need to see you. Please call me," Debby hung up and she sat back thinking about how stupid she was to fall for Web's lies. She felt overwhelmingly guilty by the fact that she put her son's life in harm's way all over a hard dick. How could she be so selfish? She scolded herself. The thought alone caused her to sob, eventually crying herself to sleep.

***

Web sat in his brand new 2007 burgundy Yukon Denali in front of his grandmother's building on Williams Avenue smoking a black and mild cigar while he listened to an acquaintance of his from Red Hook projects. The acquaintance was a guy Web met in Sing-Sing when Web was transferred there from Comstock after he was accused of raping a white inmate.

"That nigga Ran been asking around about you and his homework is doing well ya dig big homey?" The acquaintance said sitting with his seat reclined back.

Web blew smoke out his mouth nodding his head. "I'm saying the nigga paper long so his homework got to be efficient that's what long money does but see he don't realize my paper long and my arms stretch further than his. I'm respected city wide. That nigga a local hero, feel me?" Web grunted.

"True. Only thing the nigga know is where

you from but not where you or your old earth rest. He knows how you get down on the jux tip and he knows that you just came home. He knows what everyone knows basically." The acquaintance relayed.

"What's the price?" Web inquired.

"Fifty plus a half a square," the acquaintance informed Web on the fifty grand, half a kilo of cocaine contract on his head that Ty-Ran was gonna pay to the killer.

"Damn the nigga serious huh?" Web chuckled. "How much that nigga holding onto?"

"Son holding like a hundred squares easy. He chewing real nice in the projects and some out of town spots, Virginia, Pennsylvania and Delaware." The acquaintance said placing a CD in the trucks system. Web reclined his seat while saying, "I'm gonna end this nigga's career real soon."

***

Two days after Debby got the news of Web being responsible for her son's kidnapping she got a knock at the door. When she looked through the peephole, she became nervous seeing two suit and tie wearing white men, unmistakably police officers standing there.

"Does a Ty-Ran Clarkson live here?" One of the cops asked.

"No but I'm his son's mother, is there something wrong?" Debby asked telling herself now what?

This has been a fucked up week for me.

The cops looked at each other questionably.

"Your name is?"

"My name is Debby Clarkson," Debby answered nervously.

"Miss Clarkson did you call a man by the name of Cornelius Collins at this number?" The cop showed Debby Cornbread's phone number written on a piece of paper.

"Yes that's my friend Cornbread. Why is he in trouble?"

"No Miss Clarkson. He was found murdered in his apartment..."

Debby's mind went blank. The cop's words faded away. She became dizzy and it seemed as if everything was moving in slow motion. She didn't hear the cop ask was she okay? The next thing she knew she was being awaken by the strong smell of Ammonia. She was lying in her couch with her son crying over her with the two cops that knocked on her door.

"What happened? Baby stop crying." Debby said feeling dizzy.

"Miss Clarkson when was the last time you spoke to Cornelius?" Then Debby remembered they just told her Cornbread was dead. Debby screamed.

Chapter 10

Deidre

For the first time in her life, Liz questioned her gut feeling about something. Any other time her gut instincts were on point. *Maybe Debby was right, maybe I am paranoid,* Liz thought.

She and Deidre have been the best of friends since they were knee-high girls who played with dolls together, tag and other games children played back in the day. Games kids these days don't play. Liz felt bad letting a gut feeling over a man come between their friendship a friendship that stood the test of time. They had went through heartbreaks together, deaths of relatives and friends, Deidre and her parents became a second family to Liz when Liz's home became extremely dysfunctional. So when Deidre told Diondre that she would close up the salon then mouthed to Liz that they needed to talk, Liz couldn't of felt more relieved. She loved Jabbar but not enough to come between her and the woman that helped her change her life for the better. When Deidre closed the salon, she and Liz stood under umbrellas and stepped out into the rainy night. The streets of Bruekelen projects were dark and empty.

"Where we going Dee?" Liz yelled over the rumble of thunder. Deidre looked around trying to figure that out herself. Then she gave Liz a mischievous grin. "Let's go ride the train like we did when we were kids."

"Girl you crazy," Liz smiled. Still they both walked to the 105th street train station and boarded a Manhattan bound L train.

"That wind blew my damn umbrella, look at my hair," Deidre said looking at her wet hair in the window of the moving train. "Looks like you'll be doing my hair tomorrow," Deidre said looking at Liz reflection in the mirror. Liz held on to the pole staring at Deidre.

"Deidre I love you," Liz snorted. Deidre turned to look at Liz with a confused expression.

"I love you too Liz. Please don't tell me you're dying," Deidre said worried.

"Why would you think that? No I ain't dying," Liz said shaking her head.

Deidre exhaled. "Good. You almost had me thinking the way you've been acting lately was from depression."

"And I'm sorry Deidre for the way I've been acting. Just so much has been going on lately. This thing with Debby, being in love and working at the shop; it's all happening so fast. And I don't know Dee but you act like nothing bothers you like your either not human or your holding something back and don't feel I'm a friend enough to talk to about things." Liz didn't wanna accuse Deidre of trying to steal her man so she tried a different approach to get Deidre to talk. Maybe Deidre would admit that she's guilty of having an attraction to Jabbar.

Deidre didn't realize that she appeared to be the way Liz was saying she was. Since the opening of the salon, they haven't talked or spent a lot of time together like they use to and Deidre felt bad. She just didn't know it affected Liz that way.

"I didn't know that I seemed to be straying away from our friendship. Never in a million years would I not be a shoulder for you. You know you can come to me about anything. Liz I love you, you're my sister, my best friend and that will never change." The two women hugged each other in the empty subway cart as raindrops echoed from slamming against the train.

"I'm partly to blame too. I've been spending a lot of time with Jabbar and not asking you to hang with me. I'm sorry," Liz blurted.

Deidre waved her off. "Girl we're getting older. Our lives are changing, were not those little girls running around the projects playing run-catch-kiss with the boys. Were running, catching and fucking our men now and planning to have families of our own." The women laughed.

"Let's just promise to grow up and not grow apart," Liz said.

Deidre held out her hand for Liz to shake. "Agreed."

"Now let's ride to 42nd street and go play video games," Deidre said in childish voice.

"Bet," Liz answered childishly. They rode the forty-five minutes ride laughing and talking as they did since their youth.

When Diondre got home that night he got out

of his car and noticed two white men wearing trench coats, one had a fedora while the other had a full head of gray hair walking up the steps of his Fort-Greene Brownstone.

"Excuse me are you looking for someone?" Diondre asked walking up the steps holding an umbrella.

The white haired one spoke while flashing his badge. "Bronx homicide and your name is?"

Diondre confused and frightened wondered why two homicide detectives would be at his door. Frightened cause he hoped nobody in his family gotten killed or Deidre. Then he realized the cops said Bronx homicide. The Bronx?

"My name is Diondre Taylor. What is this about?"

"Mister Taylor are you kin to or associated with a man name Cornelius Cornbread Collins out of the Bronx?"

The first thing that came to Diondre mind was what Cornbread did. *I know this boy ain't kill nobody or get himself involved in no murder,* "Yeah that's a friend of mines. Is he in some sort of trouble?" Diondre looked at both Detectives faces. He couldn't read their expressions. He figured from the ages they appeared to look, that they were veterans who seen it all heard it all.

"Mister Collins is deceased. He was found murdered in his Bronx apartment."

"What...Murdered... Nah man I was just with him. When did this happen?"

The detectives informed Diondre that it was

the night that he and Cornbread hung out at his apartment and bowled in White Plains.

"We need you to come to the station Mister Taylor. We have something we want you to look at," the detectives said.

"Right now?" Diondre asked still in shock from hearing the news of Cornbread's murder. He pictured in his mind Cornbread lying dead in his Co-op city apartment. Diondre was choked up.

"Yes now Mister Taylor," the detective said matter of factly.

"I have to call my girlfriend so she won't be worried and she has to open up our salon in the morning. I know it's gonna be a long night." Diondre dialed Deidre cell phone number. He became angry when her voice mail was activated. "Goddamn voice mail!" Diondre sighed."Okay let's go."

The detective didn't want to inconvenience Diondre by bringing him to the Bronx precinct they worked out so they brought him down to the local precinct. Once there they sat Diondre in a dirty interrogation room that smelled like stale cigarettes and body funk. Besides the graffiti marked table, there was a twenty-seven inch television sitting on a stand that also had an old dusty VCR under it.

"Mister Taylor we're gonna show you some surveillance videos. We're tryna come up with a time frame and when this homicide occurred." The gray haired detective said as he placed a video cassette in the VCR all the while Diondre thinking, *they still make and use those?*

When the very clear surveillance video came

on Diondre recognized him and Cornbread leaving his Co-op city building.

"That's me and Bread," Diondre pointed the detective paused the video.

"Okay Mister Taylor I'm gonna fast forward this to where ya'll entered the garage and left. Tell me, where did ya'll go from there?"

"We went bowling in White Plains. We were there for at least an hour and a half," Diondre answered.

"Between that time did Mister Collins stop to speak to anyone, an argument or anything. Put it like this, do you know of enemies he may have that would want him dead?" the detective asked sitting down with a pen and pad.

Diondre relayed to the cops that he and Cornbread had just started hanging after years of not seeing each other. He didn't know what Cornbread was into and didn't know who he associated with.

"We were just childhood friends catching up on old times." After about four hours of questioning, the detectives offered Diondre a ride home. Diondre declined. "I need to take a walk. Thanks but no thanks."

Diondre walked down the tree-lined streets of Fort-Greene in deep thought. He thought about Cornbread. *"Why?"* Was the question Diondre asked. *"Why does the goods one have to go as tragically?" "Why do men like Cornbread risk their lives for a dollar they could make honestly?" "Why do black men place more value on material items than their own lives?"*

Tears rolled down his face as he pondered the many questions that seem to have no answer. Then he thought about Debby. As soon as Cornbread starts messing with her, he gets killed. Diondre wondered if there was a link. Why was there so much bad luck when it came to her? Was it a coincidence that her son was just kidnapped for ransom with people suspicious of her involvement and the murder of Cornbread? The more he thought about it the angrier he became.

Diondre didn't want to go home with this much hurt and anger on his mind and having to probably wake Deidre up with all this bad news. He didn't want to take his frustration out on anyone so decided to go to a diner for something to eat. He checked his voice mail and when he heard Deidre's message he became more frustrated.

"Baby me and Liz are pulling a all nighter. I'll see you at the shop in the morning. Goodnight love."

Diondre could hear the laughter of Liz in the background. While they were out having a good time, his friend was laying in a cold box with a tag on his toe dead. Could it get any worse? Diondre asked himself. It can and it most surely will.

Deidre spent a night at Liz's house reminiscent of their childhood sleepovers. They stayed up talking about everything from, clothes, hairstyles, famous men they found sexy and fantasized about sleeping with, their sex lives both describing their significant others sexual prowess all while eating cookies and drinking warm milk.

The next morning they woke together with

Liz making them some breakfast. After showering, they walked to the shop thinking that Dre would have already opened up. The store was closed.

Just as Deidre was reaching in her purse for her cell phone, Dre drove up in his 06 black Durango.

Deidre noticed the bags under Dre's eyes and the stubble on his face. He looked like he had a rough night. "I was just about to..." Deidre was cut off by Dre's menacing look at her and Liz. He pointed an accusing finger at Liz.

"I don't want that bitch Debby nowhere near this place ever again. If she needs her hair done you do it somewhere else but I don't want her as close as ten feet from this door and I mean every damn word of it. She never steps in this place as long as I'm breathing. If you don't like what I'm saying you can find another place to work!"

As Diondre pulled the keys out of his pocket, Liz stood dumbfounded as did Deidre. "Dre what happen?" Deidre asked.

"Either that woman has a curse on her of bad luck or an omen, or she is just trifling, but bad things happen when you deal with her and I don't want it around me," Dre barked opening the gate to the salon.

"Dre what did she do?" Liz finally spoke.

"Cornbread got killed. That's what. He starts fucking her and now he's dead," Diondre snarled. Liz covered her mouth and started to back away from Deidre and Diondre.

"Oh no please no. Tell me it ain't true!" Liz

cried then she ran towards her building. Deidre stood frozen. She didn't know what to say. She didn't want to frustrate Dre anymore than he was so she stayed silent. The same way she did when Dre found out about Shamar. She would wait for when Dre wanted to talk about it and when he did, she would be all ears and warms shoulder to lean on. Until then she let her tears fall. Her tears weren't just for Cornbread, but for the thousands of young black men who were murdered on the mean streets of America's urban jungles and for the mothers and families of these slain men and children caught in the middle of the madness.

Liz ran into her apartment crying. She used her cell phone to make a call. When the person picked up Liz cried. "Jabbar I need to see you baby." Jabbar sounded concern replying, "Baby what's wrong. Talk to me."

"I just need to be with you right now. I need you to hold me and tell me everything is going to be all right."

"Okay baby I'm coming right now. We'll talk when I get there. Stop crying."

"Hurry up," Liz cried then hung up. She looked at her phone and dialed another number.

Debby picked up on the first ring. She knew it was Liz from her caller ID.

"Liz?" Debby sounded as if she were crying.

"Debby?"

"Liz somebody killed Cornbread," Debby cried.

"Debby please tell me you didn't have

anything to do with it. Please don't lie to me Debby tell me you didn't!" Liz sobbed. All Liz heard was Debby drop her phone and scream.

"Nooooo!"

Chapter 11

Debra

A Month Later

Since the revelation of Cornbread's murder and the subsequent wake and funeral held in the Bronx, Liz or Debra hadn't spoken or seen each other. At the funeral Liz along with Jabbar, Deidre, Diondre and Cornbread's father, who was a shadow of his former self having lost almost half his one-hundred and eighty pounds and his hair, stood on opposite sides of the casket from Debby. Even Diondre's parents and sister flew to New York to support Diondre in his mourning.

The week of the funeral, Diondre paid tribute to Cornbread by closing the shop. Jabbar stayed by Liz's side through the ordeal. He slept at her apartment that whole week. He cooked, cleaned and even bathed Liz while staying there. Liz couldn't have asked for a better man.

After Liz's phone call to Debby asking her to tell her she didn't have anything to do with Cornbread's murder, Debby tried to get in contact with Liz. She left a message on her voice mail and answering machine pleading to Liz stressing the point that she had nothing to do with Corn-bread's murder but Liz knowing that Debby was capable of pulling a stunt like that, felt Diondre's words had credence to it. Too many bad things were happening around Debby.

Though the police have yet to come up with a suspect or clue as to who was responsible for Cornbread's demise, the streets primary suspect was Debby setting him up. So Liz never responded to Debby's calls or messages. She wanted to, out of curiosity but she didn't want anyone suspecting her of conspiring with Debby so she chose to fall back until the truth came out.

At the shop, things were slowly getting back to normal except for Diondre's attitude. His face was always in an expression of seriousness and hurt. He barely spoke to any of the employee's except to collect money or listen as someone explain why they needed some time off.

His response would be, "Sure take as much time as you need." The Diondre of the days before Cornbread's murder would have been concerned with why the employee needed the time off. "Is everything all right? Do you need to talk about it? Anything I can do?" would have been his response.
Deidre was her normal self again. She was a patient woman. She would explain to everyone at the shop out of earshot of Diondre that Diondre will be back to the Diondre we all know and love, just be patient as she was. Hell, she had to live with him.

One night when Deidre and Liz hung out at Liz's apartment Deidre said, "I never thought I would ever hear these words from Diondre but he said he was ready to leave Brooklyn. In fact New York period."

"Why?" Liz asked.

"The same reason his family left. They said it's a depressing city. More bad happens than good. Oh and it's expensive." Deidre answered.

"And you know what Liz? I'm starting to feel the same way. I feel if I don't get away things are gonna keep happening and it's just gonna get worst," Deidre continued sounding depressed.

"I feel you, but I love Brooklyn Dee. My whole life is here. I know it hasn't been a great life but when it's good here it's real good. There's nothing boring about Brooklyn. I can't imagine living nowhere where there's no drama. What don't kill you will only make you stronger," Liz preached.

"I bet you if Jabbar wanted to leave your ass would be packed in a New York minute,"

Deidre joked.

"And you know this man," Liz did a mock of Chris Tucker in the movie Friday.

***

As inconspicuous as Debby tried to appear while stuffing her Louis Vutton back pack laced with aluminum foil taped in the whole inside with clothing from off the racks in a Bloomingdale's located in midtown Manhattan, she was spotted by a security personnel.

He watched Debby for at least thirty minutes roaming around from section to section stuffing expensive clothing in her bag. Debby never noticed him because he didn't wear a uniform and he blended in with other customers.

He kept himself at a distance enough for Debby not to become suspicious of him, and he already alerted personnel that watched the surveillance cameras to keep the eye in the sky on her.

Their plan was to wait for her to try and leave the store because if they stopped her prematurely she could claim she was taking them to the counter to be purchased and had to put some in her bags because she couldn't hold all of them in her hands.

When Debby was satisfied that she had enough she made her way towards the exit. The young security guy walked behind her. He told himself, once he got a good look at her backside, Damn if I wasn't about to catch her for stealing I would try to get with her. Her backyard is tryna bust out them jeans. He grabbed his crotch looking at that rump bounce as she cat-walked towards the exit.

"Excuse me Miss," he called out to her in a smooth voice. Debby turned to see where the voice was coming from. When she saw his face, she immediately thought it was some young cat mesmerized by her ass trying to get some rap.

"I don't have time shorty. Plus you look a little too young for me," she smiled at him.

Then she felt someone grab her arm, she turned and looked in the face of a tall, huge clean faced white man.

"Ma'am we need you to come with us," the young black man said. Debby was not only frightened but she was embarrassed. People saw what was happening and stop to see the scene.

Young group of teens laughed and Debby heard one of them comment, "She got bagged. She is going to jail."

"Come where, why ya'll grab me for. What cause I'm black?" Debbie started barking.

"No ma'am your blackness has nothing to do with those stolen items in your bag," the young black security guy said with a smile.

Debby was taken into a small office where she was locked in until the cops came. The security personnel removed the items from the bag, and wearing gloves to preserve fingerprints that Debby may have left on the hangers of some, they placed them in brown paper bags.

Meanwhile in Red Hook projects Ty-Ran left his son with his mother while he walked outside to congregate with some of his homeys standing on the corner where he parked his Maserati.

"A yo what's up dude? Yo see if you recognize this blue car that keeps riding around here." One of Ty-Ran's homeys wearing a crispy white t-shirt and baggy jeans and white on white air forces said after giving Ty-Ran a five and a handshake that Ty-Ran and his crew made up in their own style.

"The windows are tinted. I don't know if its police or not but I ain't never see it before," another homey said in passing Ty-Ran a lit blunt. They were all facing the street as they stood in front of a bodega that was blasting Spanish music. In the distance, the sound of an ice cream truck could be heard mixed with the voices of children playing in the project playgrounds and in front of buildings.

"Ya'll niggas puffing on this sour diesel got ya'll out here, paranoid," Ty-Ran said still alert to every car passing by. He was interrupted by his phone vibrating on his hip. He looked at the caller ID and it didn't give a name. "Yo who dis?" Ty-Ran said into his phone still looking at every car that drove down the street.

"Ran it's me." Ty-Ran recognized Debby's voice.

"What's up?"

"Ran I got locked up. I'm in the city," Debby mumbled.

Ran had to stop himself from laughing out loud. "What you locked up for?"

"I got caught stealing shit in Bloomingdales. Ran you know this ain't my first time and they going to give me a bail. Can you please come get me," Debby begged.

"Yo you stupid. Why you always call me when this shit happens? What do you be fucking all these other niggas for? Get something out of it instead of a face full of nut," Ran scolded. Debby got angry but she knew she had to bite her tongue. Now wasn't the time to get into an argument.

"1 know Ran I ain't got nobody else to call. Don't leave me here our son going be crying asking where I am thinking I left him," Debby used the son card hoping that would motivate Ty- Ran. She knew Ty-Ran didn't want to get stuck with the responsibility of raising a child. He had two other babies that he barely saw or spent time with.

"You should of thought about that when you were being a thief asshole," Ty-Ran was enjoying putting her down. He knew she wouldn't beef because she needed him now. Any other time she would of cursed him out and hung the phone up.

"What's your bail?"

"I ain't get one yet they running me through the system now. The courthouse is on 100 Centre Street. Please Ran come get me."

"Aight stupid I'll either send somebody or I'll come. I'm out," Ty-Ran hung the phone up.

Laughing he turned to his crew and blurted. "Yo my son's mom locked up in the city for boosting."

"You talking bout the one with the fat ass from Canarsie?" A homey asked.

"Yeah her dumb ass," Ty-Ran answered.

"Son go get her, ain't no sense of all that ass being in no jail." They all howled in laughter.

Ty-Ran and his boys stood on the corner for a couple of hours. Some selling drugs while others smoked weed, talked animated on different topics, mostly girls who they had sexed or wanted to sex. They spoke about past beefs and future beefs in and out of the neighborhood and about guys who were on locked down from some of those beefs.

"Yo Ran I got a kite from Mook," one of Ty-Ran's homies pulled him to the side out of earshot of the other guys.

"Word? What he talkin' bout, he get that paper

I sent him?" Ty-Ran asked while looking at his Breitling watch.

"I talked to him about what he knew about dude the homo nigga Web. He said he know son. They were in the bing together up in Greenhaven. He said he could reach out to dude and squash it and get the paperback but if its pass that you gotta act now cause dude ain't nothing to play with on these streets."

Ty-Ran shrugged his shoulders. "And what am I a joke? Yeah it's beyond getting squashed that nigga nap my seed son. Fuck I look like letting that slide and who the fuck is Mook to send word to the street for dude to give me my paper back? This nigga an old nigga, Mook younger than me," Ty-Ran said sounding aggravated.

"Mook got status in the mountains with the real right," the homie relayed to Ty-Ran letting Ty-Ran know that Mook was a ranking member of the bloods in the prison system.

"So the old nigga blood?" Ty-Ran inquired. The homey shrugged his shoulders before responding. "I don't know, Mook ain't say."

Ty-Ran laughed before walking off. "I know them niggas up north ain't got any faggots blood, fuck is this world coming to. I gotta go pick this dumb chick up. I'll holla."

Ty-Ran walked into the street to enter his Maserati from the driver's side. Suddenly out of nowhere, the sound of a speeding car could be heard and before Ty-Ran could move. Boom! The car hit Ty-Ran sending him almost ten feet in the air half a block up the street. His tan timberland, along with his large necklace flew off his body landing near a sewer. The guys on the corner looked in shock. Some reached in their pants for guns as they saw the car that hit Ty-Ran stop near Ty-Ran's body, which was twitching. Web wearing a black pilot jacket, black jeans and boots with a black and white sox fitted cap pulled down over his eyes got out the car and aimed a .357 Desert Eagle at Ran's body. Boc! Boc! Boc! He put three bullets in Ran's head. Ty-Ran's homeys begin shooting at Web. Boc! Boc! Booom! Boom! Pow! Pow! Web was already back in the car driving off when the shots from the corner rang out.

When Ty-Ran homeys ran over to him they knew from the way Ty-Ran's eyes was shot out and what look like brain matters spilling out from under his head that Ty-Ran was dead. The fact was he was dead before the bullets hit him. The sound of people screaming and running and the sirens in the background alerted the crew that they had to flee the area. One of them went in Ty-Ran's pocket of his jeans and removed a set of keys. He skipped over to Ty-Ran's Maserati, got in; and with the voice of the Rapper styles P. blasting out the speakers, he sped off.

***

"Your honor the people ask that bail be set at five thousand cash five thousand bond. The defendant has prior convictions for the same crime, she is a habitual offender."

Debby stood next to her lawyer with tears in her eyes after she noticed no one was in the court waiting to hear her bail. When she got to a phone, she was going to curse Ty-Ran out. He wanted her to sit in jail. This was funny to him.

"Your honor that's a bit high. The defendant is a single mother who is unemployed collecting public assistance. This isn't a violent crime your honor," Debby's legal aid snarled.

The female judge a middle-aged white woman looked at Debby over her wire-rimmed glasses.

"As a mother you should be ashamed of your behavior. If you continue this criminal behavior you'll eventually lose the right to be a parent and that's worst than any sentence you can receive. I'm setting bail at fifteen hundred cash. Next case!"

When Debby was placed back in the bullpen awaiting a bus to bring her and the other women to Riker's Island she called Ty-Ran. When she got his voice mail she slammed the phone down.

"Motherfucka!"

After about a minute or two, Debby picked the phone back up and reluctantly dialed a number. Desperate times call for desperate measures. She thought. "Web, I need your help please."

Chapter 12

Diondre

Answering the doorbell with a cotton robe on over a two piece pajama set, Deidre face became flustered when she opened her door and saw Jabbar standing there dressed in a wonderfully fit rustic brown suit from the Steve Harvey Collection.

"Hey Jabbar what brings... uh I mean," Deidre was at a loss for words. Jabbar looked at his watch.

"I was supposed to meet Diondre here. Did he forget?" Jabbar smiled.

"Oh that's right I'm sorry come on in. Diondre ran to the store real quick he should be back any minute now," Deidre said while walking up a hall with Jabbar behind looking at the robe and how Deidre's plump end bounced in it. Her ass wasn't huge but it was nice and plump.

"I don't know why sisters wear makeup cause ya'll don't need it. Your skin already has a wonderful color. Look at you, your beautiful without makeup," Jabbar commented as he sat at the kitchen table. His cologne, whatever kind it was smelled delightful and made Deidre skin goose bump.

"I'm going to get in the shower. Do you want something to drink coffee, tea, did you have breakfast?" Deidre said in a fast pace sounding nervous after blushing from Jabbar's compliment.

"I'm fine thank you. I had breakfast a half hour ago," Jabbar replied.

"Ok make yourself at home. Diondre will be here any second," Deidre said and just as she was walking up the steps she heard the door being opened and in walked Diondre.

"Hey Jabbar what's up. I just ran to the store. You weren't here long were you?" Diondre asked taking off a thin jacket he was wearing.

"No Deidre just let me in a few seconds ago."

Deidre went upstairs and instead of taking a hot shower, which was her usual routine. She took a cold one. An hour later she came down the stairs fully dressed in a skirt that hugged her curves and wore her hair in a bun with no makeup on. Diondre and Jabbar were in the living room where Diondre had a portrait size picture of Elijah Muhammad leaned against the fireplace with his built in wall safe exposed.

"This is some real state of the art stuff here Jabbar. Cost me a pretty penny I never trusted banks or nothing like that," Diondre was saying.

"Well I'm telling you, you can trust these investment firms, it worked for me," Jabbar was saying with his white shirt sleeves rolled up showing his muscular forearms where Deidre noticed a lot of tattoos that looked like amateur tats. More like jail house tats.

"You said you started with Scott trade, their rates are seven to eight dollars a trade. Then you moved to Charles Shwabb and you made twenty grand in one year just off of shares of Texas instruments?" Diondre asked in amazement.

"Exactly I can show you my portfolio. I'll bring it to the shop tomorrow," Jabbar said with conviction.

Deidre smiled. There's nothing sexier than business minded black men who looked real good.

"No I believe you broker. I'm just amazed. I didn't know the market was so profitable," Diondre said.

"A lot of our people don't. It's something that's not instilled in us early on. When I was growing up in Park Slope, I never heard anyone discuss stocks, mutual funds, CD's, bonds or nothing of that nature. I never seen Wall street until I was in my twenties and that's when I got a job as a messenger," Jabbar commented.

"Well I'm on my way to the shop. I'll leave you investors and financiers alone," Deidre joked as she grabbed her keys off the kitchen table.

"Tell Liz I'll see her tonight," Jabbar said.

"Will do, will do," Deidre said merrily.

"So how much should I invest from the beginning?" Diondre asked.

"To see a large profit you wanna go large but you don't wanna throw all your eggs in one basket. Whatever you got that you could afford to play with without it being a burden on your bills, car payments you know what I mean?" Jabbar said.

"The shop has been turning over a good profit plus I had money saved up for a while. My parents started a trust for me when I was a kid. I got like a good seventy grand I can do what I like with. What you think?" Diondre said sounding elated.

Jabbar shrugged his shoulders. "Go for it. I'll show you how to get started. Give me a minute to get in contact with the right people. You're gonna need a broker and a broker you can trust, so I'll get on that ASAP." Jabbar said. Afterwards they shook hands then sat down to watch a basketball game on Diondre's sixty-inch plasma television.

***

The only thing on Debby's mind as she sat on the bed of a sleazy motel in Chinatown was getting this whole ordeal over with. She wanted to go home to be with her son and call Ty-Ran and give him a piece of her mind. Until then she has to deal with a man she has come to despise.

BROOKLYN SEXY PART 1

ABOUT THE AUTHOR

Myles Ramzee describes himself as, a "tale of two boroughs" born in Brooklyn, New York raise in the streets of Jamaica Queens and Brooklyn. Growing up in a Muslim household Myles parents instill in him manners, discipline and respect for himself and others. Life hasn't always been easy for him both parents were former drug addicts they separated when he was at the age of 6. As Myles reached his teenage years he searched for a father figure he turned to the streets to find one in hustlers and gangsters that ran his neighborhood. Myles constantly struggles within himself the battle of being a hoodlum and being a righteous Muslim.

Once his mother became a fully fledged lesbian she and her manipulative lover sold drugs. Myles mother constantly scolded him for staying in the streets. That's what pushed Myles further into the streets. Myles sold drugs on the streets of South Jamaica. He also robbed and sold drugs on the streets of Brooklyn that cause him to go in and out of jail.

At the age of 23 years old Myles life change forever when the U. S. Marshalls came and raided his Bruekelen apartment for a murder of a man who was associated with a friend of his. Myles eventually was locked up in Pennsylvania for a murder he didn't commit and was falsely accused. He was framed and evidences were manufactured along with deceit and lies of a female Caucasian drug addict who implicated him and three of Myles friends in the crime. An all white jury in Carbon Country, Pennsylvania found him and his friends guilty and sentence them all to life without parole. Presently Myles continue to fight for his innocence and his freedom.

Myles has completely changed his life for the better good. He is actively involved in a mentor program where he and several other men incarcerated lecture teens to keep them on the right track.

BROOKLYN SEXY PART 1

Myles Ramzee Other Books

BROOKLYN SEXY PART 2 $10.99

In almost every city in America, women are stereo typed based on the sections or neighborhood they came from. The five boroughs of New York City are like five different cities in one. They are close in proximity and in a lot of ways they are worlds apart.

Brooklyn, the most populated borough, probably has the city's worst reputation when it comes to people, in particular to men of the boroughs. Brooklyn women have the reputation of being seen tough, mean spirited and conniving money hungry thieves who set up men to be robbed by Brooklyn stick up kids. Diondre, a Brooklyn born and raised entrepreneur has two best friends from Harlem who feel as if all Brooklyn women fit the stereotype. Diondre sets out to prove them wrong.

When Diondre meets Deidre, a girl he met in high school. Deidre knocks the stereotype out of Prospect Park. Sadly one of Diondre's best friends doesn't live to see it. The mean streets of Brooklyn claim his life to which the other friend develops a disdain for the borough known as, "Buck Town."

As Diondre defends Brooklyn women he is shocked to find out that his woman is exactly what his friends claim Brooklyn women are like. Deidre's deep dark secret comes to light. He learns this heart breaking news at the cost of a close friend life. Brooklyn Sexy Part 1 and 2 is a tale of betrayal, infidelity, sex, robbery, karma, murder and love. It's truly a Brooklyn Story.

FLIPPIN' THE GAME 3   **$15.99**

After the convictions and deaths of the Black Top Crew hierarchy, Keenan Giles Junior sets out to clear his family name and build a relationship with the last of the Classon clan, Malik. Malik, now more mature and meeting the love of his life wants out of the game. Keenan Junior thinks Malik is getting weak and seeks to get rid of all the Classons will not let another family member tarnish the bloodline.

Enjoy these other books. Urban Fiction at its best.

SOUTH PHILLY CHICK 1 (The Epitome of Loyalty)   **$15.99**

Tina Tee White take you through the journey of her life as a young black girl, into her adult years as a South Philly chick, going through stages of three lovers tied to a life of crime. From burglary, to shop lifting, credit card scams, drug abuse, robberies, set ups, and murders, she lives it all.

She meet the love her life, Mar. Their love affair can be viewed in the pages of a fairy tale (with murders and kidnapping). Tee brings to life the myth of the South Philly Chick. Through her loyalty, trust, and unconditional love for her man; a ruthless and psychopathic murderer; they exemplify the Hood's new Bonnie and Clyde. But will they live happily ever after? You'll find out, but not in the first of this trilogy.

SOUTH PHILLY CHICK 2: (The Keys to the City) $15.99

Once again, Mar and Tee, South Philly's King and Queen return. After being saved by Mar, life goes on. The city of Philadelphia's underworld is given to Mar on a silver platter, but with that platter comes betrayal, death and deceit.

Mar tries his hand at something new. La Cosa Nostra boss Don Salvatore Bellini will give Mar the keys to the city. Will this historical event be a successful one?

When the riches are presented, hatred, jealousy, envy and betrayal are sure to follow it.

Once again, Tee proves to be the epitome of loyalty like the ride or die chick she is. If you enjoyed Volume I, you will love Vol. II. Now sit back and enjoy the ride of one of the hardest street savvy visionaries. Big Snoop doesn't just write, he recollects!

Millennium Black Millionaires $15.99

The city of Philadelphia is flood with ruthless gangsters and killers. The infamous M.B.M. family goes from being dead broke hustling in the streets to living a lavish life style that is only seen in the movies.

Everything changes for them when Sasaladine meets Alicia and she introduces him to corporate hustling. Just as they start making the transition from the streets to go corporate, their past come back to haunt them and Sasaladine is arrested for a homicide.

Franchise is the loose cannon of the crew and will kill at the drop of a dime. He has his own plans on taking over the streets of Philly by force but he runs into a problem with Tameka and Mario, two females that are just as trigger happy as him and are ready for war.

Rasul and Naim work hard at trying to leave the street life alone but can't resist splurging on nice things now that they have money.

They are all taken by surprise when the F.B.I. moves in and arrest a key member of the M.B.M. and puts everything that they worked hard for at risk.

Will they be able to live out their dreams or will they spend the rest of their days in Federal lock up? You will find out but not in the first of a trilogy.

Millennium Black Millionaires 2: The City of Brotherly Love $15.99

The Millennium Black Millionaires are back by popular demand. Marlo and Tameka are up to their old tricks again when they head to the Bad Landz looking for a new place to distribute their cocaine. An all about war occurs when they bump into Belinda and Maidi two Spanish females with just as much money and heart as them.

Alicia and Babia start to learn their way around Philly and fall in love with the upbeat pace of the city while Kasha and Patrice work hard at trying to be successful but loses focus once Rasheeda introduces them to credit card scams.

Just when they start to see life changing results. Everything comes to a halt and one of the girls is killed during a botched robbery. Will the girls be successful at finding the right loop holes in the streets?

You will find out but not in the second book of the trilogy.

BLACK OPT'S DIVISION (BETRAYAL) DECEIT OF THE HIP-HOP WORLD $15.00

Black Opt's Division takes you deep inside Philadelphia's underworld of drugs, dope-money and murder. It exposes the hidden agenda of certain government branches and their insincerity of intentions towards the African American race. Yet it's filled with enough swagger for "Hollywood." This book will captivate the mind with its intense violent scenes and exquisite sex scenes.

While exposing the F.B.I. conspiracy with drugs in Philadelphia, it explains how Feds manipulate the streets with informers. Last but not least, the romance love scene between J-Sizzle and Kema will leave you in tears. A tale of sex, murder, Hip-Hop, bad bitches and coke.......

More Great Reads Coming Soon

Millennium Black Millionaires 3
South Philly Chick III
Heir To The Throne Trilogy
DA-M (Born to Win) The Realest Hood Tale Neva Told

Mail This Order Form to:

Angel Eyes Publications
P. O. Box 22031
Beachwood, Ohio 44122

	QTY	PRICE
Brooklyn Sexy Part 1	_____	$10.99
Brooklyn Sexy Part 2	_____	$10.99
Flippin' The Game 3	_____	$15.99
Millennium Black Millionaires 1	_____	$15.99
Millennium Black Millionaires 2	_____	$15.99
Black Opt's Division Betrayal	_____	$15.99
South Philly Chick I	_____	$15.99
South Philly Chick II	_____	$15.99

Add 3.95 for each book for Shipping and Handling
We ship to prisons... State, County and Federal

Name_____

Address _____

State_____ City_____ Zip _____

Angel Eyes Publications and H. S. P. Publications
Thank You For Your Business

BROOKLYN SEXY PART 1

CPSIA information can be obtained at www.ICGtesting.com
Printed in the USA
LVOW04s2240290715

448121LV00010B/179/P

9 780692 285978